I Be Happy

by
Linda Bearer Tuttle

Pathways of Lights, Inc.

Other Books by Linda Bearer Tuttle

Sacred Search for Sanity: Spiritual Psychotherapy

Dedication

For my children,
who have shared with me
the true meanings of life, laughter, and love.
You are each unique and special.
God did His perfect work the days you were born.

Acknowledgments

First and foremost, I want to thank Ed Tuttle, my amazing and wonderful husband and best friend. He remained a constant in my life and like the northern star, he never allowed me to get lost, even during the darkest nights. He encouraged me to write this story and kept faith in my ability to complete it.

To the Word Wizards, especially Spence Stimler, originator of the poem "Jaime." Spence is one of several authors who participate in the Word Wizards, a writers' group filled with remarkable and talented people, including my loving and supportive husband. They encouraged me to keep writing when I wanted to quit. They made this a better story with their questions, ideas, and suggestions. I will be forever grateful to this wonderful group of people.

Preface

When most people hear I have a child with Down Syndrome, their immediate and instinctual response is "I'm sorry." It is always an odd moment since I have no sense of sadness or loss. Having a child with special needs is different, but in many ways richer and fuller than if she had been born without Down Syndrome. I love the analogy used by Emily Perl Kingsley in her essay, "Welcome to Holland," about the experience of raising a child with a disability. She compares having a baby with special needs to planning for a trip and ending up at a different location to where you thought you were going. You can mourn that you never got to the expected destination or you can explore, appreciate, and enjoy where you are.

Jaime's life has been an incredible gift – astonishing and extraordinary. It began like many "Hero's Journeys" with the earmarks of destiny and fate. It is an epic tale of an indomitable spirit, a life of hope and love, strength and wisdom. I hope our story offers each reader the recognition that the quality of our lives is based on our attitudes and the choices we make. Often it may be difficult to choose love and happiness, but those are the choices for survival, achievement, and success. It would be selfish for me not to share her story.

While pregnant with my daughter, an acquaintance told me her mother named her brother Jaime because it meant sunshine. Hearing this, I knew that was the name I wanted for my unborn child. Years later I learned it did not mean sunshine, but rather meant to supplant (succeed, to thrive, achieve or accomplish something, to surpass). Then I realized in the French language J'aime translates to "I love." Looking back there is no name that would better describe her. Jaime is a survivor who succeeded and surpassed all expectations. She is love in action. It has been my great privilege to be her mother.

This fact-based story shares only a small portion of my life with Jaime. The events and surrounding actions have been told from my perspective. The names of many people within this story have been changed. I have done this in honor of their privacy and out of consideration that they may have a different view of their role and interactions. Other names have been left the same as a tribute to what they have done for us and in the hope that we may reconnect with them through this story.

Introduction

Jaime
By Spence Stimler

Even though I don't know Jaime
I do know Jaime
I only met her once
But I've lived a part of her life
Through her Mother's story.
At first I thought
The book was about Jaime
Then I changed my mind.
It was about Linda's problems
Coping with a handicapped child.
But I finally realized that the
Writing was about Jaime after all.
While Linda worried,
Protected, fought for, fretted,
And suffered anxiety for Jaime,
Jaime was serene in her manner.
Her seeming only concern
Was to ease the her mother's worry
Which she best expressed by saying, "I Okay."

We go through life trying to conquer
The many problems we face.
Jaime has managed
To put all the world's worries aside
She sees good in everybody and everything.
I don't think she knows how to hate.
It isn't even part of her vocabulary.
Jaime has accomplished one thing
Most of us will never know
She has been able to experience
The secret of loving.
Surely God in His Infinite wisdom
Gave her to us that we might see
Through her a small portion of His love.

— I —

In The Beginning

Flowers grow out of dark moments.
~ Corita Kent

Everything Changes

"Your baby is a bad baby." These words changed my life. They carelessly leapt from the doctor's lips and pounded on my ears, clutched at my throat, and squeezed my heart. I looked around the room for some sign this might be a joke, but the look on my husband's and parents' faces assured me this was not a joke.

People have asked what would happen if the world stopped spinning. I now know. Everything falls apart. Everything changes. Nothing stays the same. Nothing is the way you think it is, or was, or should be, or would be.

From this beginning you may believe my daughter's birth was the worst thing that could have happened to me. At that moment in time, a part of me might have agreed with you. Yet, I have learned important lessons living with Jaime. I learned that within the most unexpected and unwanted happening lie the most amazing and wonderful experiences.

There has always been a special force at work in Jaime's life. It began before she was born.

2

I want to share her story, our story, in the hope that it may help someone whose world has momentarily stopped spinning to remember everything changes.

Being pregnant for the first time was frightening. My body took on a life of its own, figuratively, and literally. I needed other people who could understand, and was thrilled to learn my best friend, Janet, was pregnant. Then another friend, Hannah, announced that she was also expecting. That is how it all started. We began meeting every week, calling ourselves the "We Three."

When Hannah, Janet and I entered our favorite health food restaurant, The Whole World, heads turned. Not because we were drop dead gorgeous, but because we were all hugely seven and eight months pregnant. We joked that we looked as if we had all gone to the same "all-night party." When people made comments, we would tell them we were triplets. Of course, none of us had similar physical features, but it was good for a laugh, and at this point in our lives we were hungry for laughter. Hannah was tall with short blonde hair and a freshly pressed look. Everything about her delivered a no-nonsense message about her approach to life. Janet was her opposite – short, with shoulder-length black hair, an easy smile and a totally carefree attitude – about everything. Me? I was the average one – medium height, with uncontrollable curly brown hair. Nothing about me stood out as memorable or spectacular.

All of us were first time mothers. When we met we compared stories about the amazing changes taking place in our bodies and our lives. Who could guess that skin could stretch this far? We had what we liked to call our "organ recitals," a time we used to discuss the aches and pains we endured which accompanied our babies' growth, as they pushed and rearranged our inner worlds, leaving no comfortable position for us to sit, stand, or even lie down.

Shifting from one uncomfortable position to another, Janet, who was the shortest and most profoundly pregnant, said, "I can't wait to have this baby!"

Her comment caused a shift in conversation and I admitted, "Sometimes I'm excited, but at other times I'm scared to death. Susan came over yesterday with Jeremy. I thought they would never leave. He wouldn't stop crying! I thought I'd go nuts! Then I thought about having my own baby and wondered what in the hell am I doing? What did I get myself into? And, how in the hell can I get out of this?!"

Janet laughed, "That's what your baby wants to know!" Using a baby voice she continued, "Help me! I don't like this mother! She doesn't love me and I'm not even born yet. Help me! Get me out of here!"

Hannah, who always seemed to be reprimanding us, solemnly said, "Janet, that's not funny. Sometimes I wonder if you're ready for this baby."

Janet gently ran her hand over her belly. "You betcha. You just come on out any ol' time you're ready. I got ear plugs."

We cracked up. We could always count on Janet. Wiping away tears of laughter, however, did not remove the shadow of doubt or fear that seemed to be ever present, lurking just beneath the surface of my being. It was so unlike me. Why couldn't I shake it? I chalked it up to the normal reaction of first pregnancy. Yet, being with the two people in the world who were most likely to understand, I tried again. "Really, I am more than a little freaked out lately. Have you two had any dreams about giving birth?"

A frown replaced the smile on Hannah's normally serene face, "I suppose you have and you're going to share it with us in vivid detail? Honestly, Linda, I don't know if I can handle that right now. The truth is, here we are – all six of us," she pats her stomach, "and we are going to be delivering soon, and there's not a darn thing we can do to change it. I don't like to think about the vivid details."

Janet, teasing Hannah, commented, "You mean like the pain of the cutting, tearing, needles, and all of that?"

We all shifted in our seats at Janet's blunt comment – my hips tightened just thinking about the impending moment. As we all slid into our personal reveries, I picked up the white cup and ran my finger around the edge, chewing on my lip. Holding it in both hands, I looked into the liquid as if it might hold some secret message. Its warmth soothed me.

Janet broke the silence, "Was your dream really a vivid dream of childbirth, Linda?"

I shook my head as a tear slid down my cheek. Hannah attempted to reach over and touch my arm. As she did this, the table tilted and we all scrambled to steady our cups. With things back in control,

Hannah said apologetically, "Okay, let's try this again. Linda, I think you need to tell us your dream."

First, looking at Hannah, I said, "You'll be relieved to know it wasn't exactly about giving birth. It was about what my baby looked like." Then I took a deep breath – I had to pause – it was just a silly dream, why was this so hard? "Okay, here it is... I gave birth to a monkey."

Hannah gasped and Janet began laughing uncontrollably. This was one of the reasons I considered Janet to be my best friend. I can count on her not to take anything too seriously and to keep me in touch with my sense of humor. Janet tugged at the corner of her sleeve, pulled it over her hand, and used it to blot the tears of laughter collecting on her cheeks. Hannah quickly reached into her purse to produce a folded pack of Kleenex. She handed one to Janet. "Really, Janet, you need to learn to be more prepared. What are you going to do when the baby comes?"

Janet quickly responded, "You mean other than getting ear plugs? I guess you'll need to stay close by to take care of us."

Hannah rolled her eyes and shook her head, knowing she was in a losing battle; they had covered this territory before.

Janet turned back to me, "I want to talk more about this dream. Did people come to visit you? Did they all keep straight faces when they told you, "'Oh, my! What a... cute... adorable baby!' You know what people always say. Although having a monkey might just give them a little trouble coming up with just the right words. 'My, oh my! What... uh... big eyes! Hey, he's really strong!' Or, 'Oh, wow! I haven't seen a baby like this one before!'"

Even Hannah, who was slightly aggravated with Janet joined in, "My goodness, look at the size of those hands, and those are the cutest ears!"

Then I decided I'd better chime in, "And I don't want you to miss his adorable feet."

We were all laughing so hard. Then my laughter turned to sobs – I couldn't stop. I could barely catch my breath. My chest hurt. My chin quivered. My hands quickly moved to cover the sounds and the sight of a mother-to-be in mortal fear of her unknown child.

Janet and Hannah immediately moved to their nurturing modes. Janet offered to take us to her home, which was nearby. I shook my head as I worked to regain composure. Using a few Kleenex to clean up the disaster area of my face after the storm, I was ready to talk again, assuring my friends, "I'm okay...really."

The first one to speak was Janet. "What is this really about, Linda?"

"I'm not sure." Shaking my head, I said, "It's not just the fears of childbirth, or the responsibilities. It feels different. I don't even think it's my hormones. But I can't shake it. I have this impending fear that something's wrong."

Hannah jumped in. "You haven't taken Thalidomide, have you?" When I shook my head, she continued, "There has been so much in the news lately about the Thalidomide babies, born without arms or legs." Janet mentioned a family friend whose baby had something wrong. But no one was sure exactly what was wrong, nor did they want to ask too many questions.

I remembered two children from my past. One was a boy who was much older, but attended our second grade class. Everyone knew he was "slow," so they made exceptions for him. He was friendly with everyone and always seemed happy, even when bad things happened like being teased by the older kids. The other child lived next door to my aunt. She must have had polio. Her leg was deformed and she was barely able walk. My aunt encouraged me to play with her. It seems so silly now, but I was terrified. I have no idea what I was afraid of, but no amount of adult reasoning could overcome my fears. My heart now hurts for my inability to befriend that lonely little girl. These memories were the foundation behind the ideas which I shared with my friends. "You know, if my child has to have something wrong, I hope it will be mental retardation. I think I can handle that."

Somewhere I heard God never gives us more than we can handle. I have often wondered if He doesn't give us advance notice when He's about to send a curve ball in our direction.

Genesis

On April 28th I woke up early, feeling great. The doctor told me last Friday I shouldn't be delivering for at least another week. Wanting to take advantage of having so much energy, I completed the normal cleaning chores and moved on to those jobs that are usually left for holidays, pre-visitors, or anger releases, such as cleaning the refrigerator and oven, or washing the walls.

Around noon my back began to object. I assured myself this was to be expected for someone who was nine and a half months pregnant. By three o'clock the pains were suspiciously different and I decided I'd better call the doctor.

He ran the gamut of rudimentary questions by me: "How long have the pains been going on? How long between? How long are they lasting?" Hearing my responses, he suggested I contact my husband, Carl, and come to the hospital as soon as he could get home. The doctor should have given other instructions, but he had no way of knowing.

Carl was never given to being overly emotional, and his first love has always been his work. Knowing that, I still expected he would be excited about this call. I had seen lots of movies about first time fathers taking their wives to the hospital. So, I tried to stay calm when I called him. Thinking back, maybe I stayed too calm. The conversation went something like this:

"Carl, I think I'm in labor. I called the doctor and he said we should come to the hospital."

"I'm in the middle of a job. I can't leave."

"But, I've been having pains for a while now and they're getting closer together."

"Linda, the doctor told you last Friday you wouldn't be delivering for at least another week. The pains are probably in your head."

"They don't feel like they are in my head. The doctor wants you to bring me to the hospital as soon as possible. What should I tell him?"

"Tell him we'll call him when I can get off, before we leave the house. I have to go now."

"Do you think you'll be home soon?"

"As soon as I can."

"Please try to... " There was a dial tone at the other end of the line.

What should I do? Pack. Pack a bag and take the necessities and things I'll want while in the hospital. The pains were only two or three minutes apart.

I began gathering things and putting them on the bed, trying to pace myself, preparing for the next shock wave. I found it reassuring to talk to myself and reminded myself to think. "What will I need? Toothbrush and toothpaste." Shoot! I had just come from the bathroom. That simple trip now seemed to take a Herculean effort to repeat.

Finally! It was four o'clock, and my bags were packed and sitting by the door. Should I call Mom and Janet and Hannah to let them know Carl was on his way home and I'm on my way to the hospital? I decided not to.

I sat and did the breathing exercises I learned at Lamaze classes. I was sure it had been several hours since I set the bags by the door. I looked at the clock, five o'clock. Should I call the doctor? What would I tell him? I felt sure Carl would be home anytime. At six, the pains increased in their intensity, each pain feeling like an earthquake, rearranging my physical being, tearing me apart. The frequency also increased to every minute or minute and a half.

Should I call my mother? I don't want anyone to know that Carl, after being told his first child was on the way, had not come home to take me to the hospital. I lay on the floor and rolled around a little, as much as a pregnant woman can roll, and moaned and cried and thought about driving myself to the hospital. But I knew I was past the point of being able to drive. Why hadn't I driven myself earlier? Because I was so sure he was going to come home. I expected him to walk in the door at any moment. Of course, I had been expecting him since four o'clock. At seven o'clock I thought of a new diversion to temporarily redirect my attention to a different part of my body. I began banging my head on the wall. It actually worked. All the stuff they say about endorphins – it really works.

Carl opened the door shortly after eight o'clock, took one look at me, and there was no doubt in his mind the pain I was experiencing was not just in my head – although I did have a fairly good size bump on my forehead from hitting it against the wall. By then I did not even have the strength to call the doctor. He began acting out the role I had so often seen in the movies – the first time father, rushing around to get his wife to the hospital. It was a little late. I hoped not too late. We were finally on our way to the hospital. I never knew the road had so many bumps. Each bump brought a groan and with each groan I was sure the baby was going to be delivered in the car.

The car pulled up to the hospital at 8:35 P.M. No one there seemed particularly excited when I arrived, even when Carl told them I was having constant contractions. There was no in-between time. I guess they always hear things like that. Seeing a panting whale of a woman, looking like she was about to burst, is a normal scene for them. They wanted all the necessary data and insurance information. The admissions clerk casually called the maternity ward to let them know we would be on our way. An aide sauntered down the hallway with a wheelchair, and proceeded along at the same pace to take me to the maternity ward. I wanted to scream at him to, "Move-it!" But I couldn't talk. All my energy was being used up in the childbirth process, panting like crazy to keep from delivering before we got to the maternity floor.

When the elevator door opened to the maternity floor the nurse did a quick assessment, and went into immediate action. "Oh, my! Honey, why did you wait so long? There's no time for prep." She quickly pushed me through the doors into the delivery room. They helped me onto the table. The anesthetist was waiting and I heard him say, "It's now or never." A calm darkness replaced the pain.

From the darkness, like a child peaking out from her bedroom and overhearing an adult conversation, I heard the nurses' voices at a distance. What were they saying? Trying to make sense of their words, I heard, "Do you think he understands?... seems too calm..." More darkness. Again the voices, "... such a shame... so young to have to deal with something like this." This time I was able to open my eyes. A woman was lying next to me. I turned. No one else was in the room. I bit my lip to see if I was awake. It hurt. This was real. They had to be talking about me or the woman next to me. I tried to talk, but no sound came out. More darkness.

"Linda," a soft voice whispered and called me back into consciousness, "We're going to take you to your room and let you sleep tonight."

I struggled with the words most important to me, "My baby?"

"You had a little girl. They had to take her to the nursery to clean her up. It's really late. It took you a long time to wake up. Your husband went home. He'll be back in the morning. You can see the doctor then. Right now you need to rest." The world went dark again.

As I woke up and moved, I was aware of a different pain than I'd had before the baby was born. Looking around, the cream colored sterile walls and the garish, flowery curtain surrounding my bed were proof enough I was in a hospital room. Someone must have thought the curtain would brighten spirits, but at the present moment, I felt like I was being attacked by a crazed flower patch. I immediately pushed the curtain back part-way, so at least, I didn't feel trapped. Just then a nurse came in carrying a baby. She didn't even look at me as she walked to the bed on the other side of the curtain. She spoke in a whispery voice to the new mother, who was coochie-cooing to her new off-spring.

As the conversation I had overheard while in the anesthetic fog snuck back into my mind, a chill ran over me. Is it possible the nurses were really talking about me? Why didn't the nurse look at me when she brought the other baby in? Why hadn't they let me see my baby last night? Where was Carl? Why hasn't anyone said anything to me about my baby?

Just then the nurse came around the curtain. She was moving quickly and was at the door when I stopped her, "Excuse me, can you bring my baby to me?"

She responded quickly with, "I'm really busy right now, but I'll check." A different nurse came to pick the baby up from the woman in the next bed. Again I asked to have my baby brought to me and told her this was my second request. I got the same answer, and again the nurse avoided looking at me.

A strange feeling started in the center of my being – like a million insects escaping from the nest and racing through my veins until they reached the ends of my fingers and toes. They then turned around and fought their way back through the frenzy of those trying to escape, causing massive internal chaos. Those nurses last night must have been talking about me. What could be wrong with my baby? I looked at my hand. It was shaking. Okay, Linda, stop it. Get control of yourself. Go down to the nursery and see your baby – they are not bringing the baby to you – you go to the baby.

Moving hurt, but not as badly as I hurt inside. Fear propelled me down the hall. I looked and guessed and prayed that I was heading in the right direction. No nurses were around. I saw the windows – there were a lot of babies. I could not see my baby. Then, I saw my parents and my husband talking to the nurse in the nursery. Now there was no doubt. They had not come to see me first. They were finding out what was wrong with the baby, before anyone told me, the mother.

What should I do? Should I bang on the window? That would surprise all of them. I should be part of their little conference. I could demand it. Tears wet my cheeks. I didn't want to let anyone see me cry. I know something they don't. I'll just go back to the room and wait. How long will it take them to tell me?

Applying make-up had special meaning as I waited for Carl and my parents. Putting on a mask, I thought, I can do this. Do what? Why hasn't anyone told me anything?

"Hi, Babe," Carl's greeting told me nothing.

"I'm glad you finally decided to see me. I can't believe you left without talking to me last night."

"They said you had a rough time and needed to sleep, and it would be best to wait until this morning."

"THEY did, did they? Who, exactly, decided that?"

"The doctor."

"Oh, I think it would have been nice to have had a chance to see the baby last night. And it would be even nicer to see her this morning. I've asked the nurses to bring her to me, but they haven't."

"Really?" I noted he was good at this covering up business.

Right then Mother and Dad walked in. This may seem like a normal happening for some families, but in my family work comes first, and it's Tuesday morning. If everything was okay, they would have come to see me after work.

I wanted to ask them what they knew. I wanted them to tell me. Why wouldn't they tell me? I decided to wait. In the control room of my mind it felt like I had one foot on the gas pedal and one foot on the brake, both pressed all the way to the floor. Our conversation was stilted, like strangers trapped in an elevator, waiting to be released. I then decided to push things and asked them to demand to have my baby brought to me.

Finally, a nurse came with the baby tightly wrapped like a burrito. Her face was so dark I wasn't sure this was the right baby. My child should be Caucasian. I didn't want to say anything, everyone seemed satisfied that this was the right baby. I reached out to take her, but the nurse said she had to take the baby immediately back to the nursery for the doctor to examine. She assured me she would bring her back later. She wouldn't even unwrap her. Were my worst fears happening? I remembered the day at The Good Place, and my conversation with Hannah and Janet. I uttered a silent prayer, "Please, God, please let my baby have arms and legs."

Dr. David Hunter strolled in at 2:00 P.M., as if the he were right on time. Carl and my parents were relieved to see him. The pretending everything was okay could finally stop. Dr. Hunter ignored my family as he came to the side of the bed and blurted out, "Linda, your baby is a bad baby."

A bad baby? What does that mean? I waited from 9:00 P.M. last night when she was born until 2:00 P.M. today, seventeen hours, to hear I have had a "bad baby?" I will not cry! I will give it back to him. So, I quickly retorted with, "What did she do? Is she taking after her mother already? She's not even twenty-four hours old. How bad can she be?" I smiled.

He didn't, but he looked a little uncomfortable, and I took some pleasure in that. "No, Linda, I mean she's a Mongoloid. Do you know what that means?"

I didn't answer, which made him look at me. I shook my head ever so slightly because if I made any major movement my entire body might fall apart. The term was vaguely familiar.

"It means she'll be retarded." After his declaration, I heard only words. The room turned into an eerie, altered existence. Nothing seemed quite real. Waves of nausea gave me a feeling of being in motion. I vowed not to cry. Maybe it was the tears filling my eyes which made everything look like I was watching a sad movie through a rain soaked window. I tried to focus on what the doctor was saying. But I was only catching every three or four of each ten or fifteen words coming from the "talking head" that released a stream of unwanted messages: retarded... not able to talk...may never walk... trouble feeding self... die early...twelve years old...and on, and on.

Suddenly, the woman in the adjoining hospital bed jumped out of her bed and drew back the curtain. Considering she had just had a baby, the speed with which she moved was nothing less than a miracle, only one of the many miracles about to happen. Her voice matched the commanding tone of the doctor's, "What you are telling her is not true!" The room fell silent.

Dr. Hunter stood erect and shook his head as if her words landed a physical blow. Their eyes locked, he cleared his throat before speaking, "I have been a doctor for more than thirty years. What would make you such an authority?"

She quietly, but firmly and calmly stated, "I teach genetics at OSU. I teach doctors like you."

"Well, you have your experience and information, and I have mine. I hope you don't mind if I finish consulting with my patient, in privacy." He nodded to the curtain. She pulled the curtain back, but not before looking at me and adding, "We can talk later." Her smile and attitude was like a seed of hopefulness planted in the desert of despair.

Dr. Hunter then said he had a doctor friend who had a "child like this," and asked if Carl and I would like to talk with him. We quickly agreed it would be a good idea since we were both feeling totally lost. As the doctor left, he sent a parting blow to my guardian angel on the other side of the curtain saying to me, "Be careful about the information you get from people who are not doctors." Having shared his wisdom, he left.

The curtain moved back again, "I guess I should introduce myself. I'm Susan. Sorry, if I made things uncomfortable by speaking up in front of the doctor. I just couldn't stand the idea that you were being given the wrong information about your baby. If you want to talk more, let me know."

And we did. I have always considered Susan to be a gift from God, which is why I refer to her as my guardian angel. In Joseph Campbell's work, "The

Hero's Journey," she would be described as the protective figure, the supernatural aide. To me she was all of this and more.

Susan helped us understand our daughter's disability. She explained about Down Syndrome being a genetic disorder. She provided updated factual information, supported by research and people who were interested and involved in the field of genetics and developmental disabilities. Susan arranged for genetic testing while Jaime was in the hospital. The results would tell us if Jaime's type of Down Syndrome was hereditary. This was important to Carl and me; it would affect decisions about our future family.

Susan was still answering questions when the nurse brought Jaime back to me. Mother, Dad and Carl took this opportunity to say goodbye. The parting words of comfort and support were accompanied with kisses and smiles that tried to deny the message in their tear-filled eyes.

Alone with the nurse, I expressed concern about Jaime's skin color. She said there was a problem with her blood which made her skin appear dark, but she also said it wouldn't last. I hesitated, but then asked the question that first came to me when I had seen her, "Are you sure this is my baby?"

She nodded and made assurances – there was no doubt. Dr. Hunter had asked her to bring Jaime and show me the features that are indicators of Down Syndrome. Jaime was quiet as she was being unwrapped. I looked at the bare child in front of me. She had arms. She had legs. She had eyes and a nose and a tiny little mouth. The nurse proceeded to point out the physical symptoms that were the indicators of Down Syndrome: the almond shape eyes, the fat pad across her back, the simian crease in her hand, the shape of a toe...but she had arms and hands and fingers, legs and feet and toes, and eyes, and ears. So she wouldn't be as smart as some people. Most people aren't half as smart as they think they are. She had arms and legs. She would be able to walk. She would be able to feed herself. She could see. She could hear.

I asked about feeding her, but the nurse said the doctor insisted she be monitored closely in the nursery right now. He only agreed to have her brought in for this brief viewing. The nurse was wrapping her and preparing to take her back when I held out my arms and said, "I want to hold her, at least for a few minutes."

Her eyes filled with tears as she tried not to look at me, "I'm sorry. I have been told, 'No.'"

"What? I'm not allowed to hold my own baby? Why?"

"Please, don't yell, I could get in a lot of trouble for telling you this. They think you may decide not take your baby home, and they don't want to make that decision any more difficult for you."

"What? What would I do with her? Of course I'm going to take her home. Give me my baby!"

The nurse stood frozen between a mother's emotional demand and a doctor's order. We were caught in a reality outside this hospital room. I do believe she was ready to hand Jaime to me when a tall thin doctor walked in, "Ah, this must be the missing baby! Hi, I'm Dr. Smith, the pediatrician."

I'm sure he must have wondered if he had a "third eye" by the incredulous look he received. But here was a man who was acting like a normal person right after I was just told the weirdest thing I had ever heard in my life. So, God bless and help this nurse, but I couldn't stop myself. I explained to the doctor what she just told me.

"Ah, I thought things seemed a little tense when I walked in. Well, I'll tell you what. I have to check this little darlin' out. That's my job. Your job is to decide if you can be her mother. We can provide you with some information which can help you. Raising a child with Down Syndrome will have more challenges than raising some children and less than others. How does that sound?"

I couldn't speak; I just nodded my head.

"Good, after I check your baby, I'll have the nurse bring her back to you, okay?"

The nurse looked uncomfortable and made a muted comment about Dr. Hunter. Dr. Smith smiled and led the way out of the room. The last thing I heard him say was, "I'll write new orders after I'm done. A baby needs a mother."

Alone again. What now? I have to tell my friends. I picked up the phone and held the receiver until I had control of myself, and I knew what I would say. I dialed Janet's number. It rang twice, maybe she won't be home. On the third ring, I was ready to hang up when she answered. I took a breath and started, "Hi. I had the ba... bab... (sobs). Janet, my baby has Down

Syndrome. It means she'll be retarded. Oh, yeah, she's a girl. (sniff)."

There was total silence at the other end of the phone, then I heard her sniffle and finally say, "Oh, Linda, I don't know what to say." I could hear panic in her voice. After all she was due to deliver any day.

"Remember, Janet, lightning doesn't strike twice. It'll be okay for you."

"God, Linda, I can't believe you are thinking about someone else at a time like this. How are you doing?"

"Okay, but Janet, it's weird. I can't connect with this baby. You know how they say mothers always have immediate mother instinct and love. I don't feel it. I don't know what I feel."

"You have just been through hell and you expect everything to be nice and neat and clear? Give yourself some time. Do you want me to call everyone for you? Would you like Hannah and me to visit?" I could always count on Janet – she would notify all of our friends and clear that path.

After I put the receiver back on the phone cradle I realized Carl and my parents had left, the doctors were gone, and my roommate was sleeping. I was alone. It was quiet, as quiet as a hospital can be. I realized how exhausted I was, but not sleepy. I sat very still. The world was swirling rapidly around me and I felt as if I was in the midst of the vortex of ... I wasn't sure what. Was this the eye of the storm? Was I headed up or down? God, how could I have had such a "normal" life up to now?

Doctor's Advice

Dr. Hunter arranged a meeting in the hospital conference room with his colleague, Dr. Williams. I was excited to hear what another parent had to say. This wasn't just another parent, he was a doctor! He would certainly have the most updated information at his disposal. Walking to the meeting I kept wondering if he would bring his wife.

I led the way into the conference room. The doctor was there by himself. I felt disappointed, but didn't want to show it. I really appreciated this busy man taking time out of his schedule to meet with us. I extended my hand and smiled as I introduced myself. He accepted my hand, but there was no life or enthusiasm as he announced, "Dr. Williams," and nodded to chairs on the other side of the table. We were not fully seated when he said, "There is no easy way to say this. If you are ever planning to have other children, do not take this child into your home."

"What? Excuse me, what did you say? I thought we were going to talk about raising a child with Down Syndrome."

"My wife and I have a fourteen-year-old daughter with Down Syndrome. We made the decision at her birth that we wanted to have other children. Knowing it would not be fair to the other children to deal with her issues, we placed her in a home. I suggest you do the same thing."

I wanted to scream, but I couldn't even speak. This was not what I had expected, nor what I wanted to hear. The room felt small and warm. His lips were moving, but I didn't know what he was saying. I focused on Carl as he asked the doctor, "Who would pay for something like that?"

"You would have to. There are different places and different price ranges. You might both have to work to afford it, but it'll be worth it."

I finally found my voice, "I'm sorry, I thought we were going to talk about raising a child at home. I don't think I could ever give my child away."

Dr. Williams didn't like my response. His face darkened. "You may have a different opinion after you live with it for a while."

"I'll think about what you've told us, but I will never call a child an it." With that I stood up and walked out of the room. I never looked back. Tears streamed down my cheeks and the hallway blurred; I wasn't sure of what direction I was going. I only wanted to put distance between myself and the doctor/father who called his child "it." What happened to the world I used to know? Sane, responsible people don't do this type of thing.

Carl tugged at my arm, "Hey, slow down. We're not in a race."

"I'm just so angry. I can't stand it! How dare he! Who does he think he is? And Dr. Hunter – wait until I get a chance to talk with him! He wants us to talk with a friend who has a child with Down Syndrome! I don't think they can call themselves parents if they've never taken a child into their home. Ooh... I am so angry!"

"I think you already said that. Maybe we should keep walking a bit before going back to the room."

"Why?"

"I'm not sure you're ready to hear this, but my parents agreed with Dr. Hunter and Dr. Williams, and they're waiting in the room."

"Well, it's a good thing you told me because I've had enough of everyone telling me what they think is best for us and our baby. What do you think?"

"It doesn't matter to me, Linda, whatever you want."

"Oh, that's just great, the biggest decision we'll ever have to make and you don't care! Well, let me tell you the first decision I am going to make. I'm going to the whirlpool bath and you can tell your parents I don't want to talk. Then let the hospital desk know I am not accepting visitors for the rest of day – and since you have no input on this decision – that includes you."

I walked away, picked up a towel at the nursing station and went directly to the whirlpool room. As my burning tears fell into the hot water which bubbled and swirled around me, I began laughing and thinking how appropriate. This whirlpool is a perfect analogy of my life – a boiling whirlpool. Hey God, am I almost done?

Another Special Event

Nurse Karen, a happy, slender, middle aged woman, had become part of my support system. She listened and didn't push me to make a decision about whether or not I should place Jaime. I was surprised when she entered my room looking especially sad. At first, I thought it might be a performance to let me know she was going to miss me since I was going home today. When she remained unhappy, I commented, "Wow! It's odd not to see a smile when you come in."

"Linda, I've been struggling with something since yesterday and I know you're getting ready to go, so it has to be now or never."

Teasing her I said, "Ah, a lady of mystery!" She still didn't smile, so I went on, "Okay, tell me what's up."

"Linda, I'll probably get in big trouble for this, but I can't help myself. You know I told you that it's rare for us to have a Down Syndrome baby born here?" I nodded. This had been part of our conversation over the past couple days.

She went on, "Well, a baby boy with Down Syndrome was born yesterday. The mother isn't handling it well. Her doctor has been telling her the same things your doctor told you. Would you be willing to meet with her, if she's open to talk? I wouldn't ask if this wasn't such an odd situation. No one here can ever remember two Down Syndrome babies being born in the same month, let alone within two days."

"You don't have to convince me. I would love to meet another parent. Let me know when."

The first meeting was arranged. Walking into the other mother's room was difficult. I chose to go by myself, and when I when I got there she was crying. I almost turned around and left. But she needed me, and the God's honest truth was I never needed another person so much in my life. I really hoped she would be open to talk. Our meeting seemed like two synchronized swimmers who needed no practice. The sharing flowed as if we were old friends who were being reacquainted after a lengthy separation.

Her name was Joyce. We were an unlikely pair. She was older, I was younger. She had been born and raised in the area, my family had moved around. Tommy was her fifth child, Jaime was my first. We had little in common, we had everything in common. We shared the pain of being told how our newborn babies have a problem. We were both told by some people, especially our doctors, that we should not take them home.

I told Joyce I was preparing to leave the hospital, without my baby. The doctor said it would be another week before Jaime could be released. But I would return each day for feedings. So Joyce and I planned to continue our sharing during those visits. I promised her I would gather information from every possible source about mental retardation, placements, and community resources.

Like every new mother, I expected to take Jaime home and have my hours filled with nurturing a new baby. But my baby's needs were different. Gathering information is how I would be tending to her while she was being cared for in the hospital. During the lonely hours ahead I would console myself with this idea.

How could I permanently place my baby when it hurt so much to leave her temporarily? Yet this question was not settled in my mind. I did not have all the facts. Taking her home was my preference, as this had been the intention from the point of conception.

Somehow I had to settle the battle that was taking place in my heart, mind, soul, and family.

Out of Place

When I left the hospital my arms were empty. My heart felt battered and bruised. It was as if I had just undergone open-heart surgery instead of having delivered a child. No woman should ever have to suffer the experience of leaving a hospital without her baby. Would Jaime still be there when I returned? Who could be trusted? Who should be believed? What should I do? These questions were my constant companions.

The road home did not seem to have as many bumps as it did on the way to the hospital. Maybe I was just numb. Carl was silent; I was silent, which was unusual. I looked out the window. The world passed by in a blur. Homes and trees seemed oddly out of shape. Hmmm...would my world ever be normal again?

We pulled into the driveway. It had been only four days, but it seemed like years. I felt so much older than the girl who left. As I walked into the living room and looked around, I saw a magazine lying on the floor with its pages twisted and torn. I must have done that while I was in labor. This house was my home, and yet I felt like a stranger, not the same person who used to live here. I had to adjust to being back. When Carl said, "I'm going to work for a while," I felt a sense of relief.

His car hadn't left the driveway when I began looking for the keys to my car. I didn't want to stay in the house. Leaving the suitcase and the bags from hospital for later, I set out on my first mission. Sitting in my car with my hands on the wheel, I began to have a sense of "being in control" for the first time since Jaime's birth. It felt good. I looked at the eyes in the rearview mirror as I got ready to back up. I was still me. I looked tired, but I was okay. I thought about the doctor saying I should take it easy and not drive for two weeks. Right. I put the car in gear and started on my journey.

Walking into a library has always provided me with a sense of peace. This library has been like a second home to me since I was nine years old, my place of wonder and magic and personal growth. I knew it would hold many of the answers I needed in my initial search for information.

Vivian, the librarian, greeted me immediately and was surprised to see me without child. A quick explanation was all that was necessary to have her direct me to a section which held a variety of books on mental retardation and Down Syndrome. She encouraged me to take as much time as I needed. In the meantime, she would find local resources for programs in the area that might be helpful. I hadn't been there three minutes when Vivian appeared again with a small stool for me to sit on. I looked at it and recognized it as a sympathy gesture; and thought about refusing it. However, politeness and exhaustion won out. I accepted it, but not without reservation. I didn't want people feeling sorry for me.

Books have always been my friends. I sat and looked at this new section and realized I had never been to this area of the library before. I wondered how many other sections I hadn't explored and thought about walking around the library to check it out. I quickly realized that would be an attempt to escape the job at hand! Shape up, Linda. Let's get on with this. I began taking books off the shelf. I had collected several when one book captured my attention. It was smaller and looked out of place. Even the name, *Many Mansions,* was different from the others in this section. Then I noted by the numbers that it was misfiled. I put it on my stack of books to give it to the librarian when I checked out so she could properly reshelf it.

My search took longer than I thought. Vivian's gentle tap on my shoulder startled me, "Are you okay?" I nodded. "We have to close now, but I'll be glad to help you carry anything you want up to the desk."

Rather than try to decide what to take, I told her I would take them all. She gathered them up and checked them out, adding the information she had gathered. I was relieved when she offered to carry all the books to my car. After loading them into the car, she turned and said, "I hope you got everything you needed." She gave me a hug and added, "You never know what you'll find at the library. Let me know if you need me to research anything else."

I was glad I had ignored the doctor's orders and felt overwhelmed with appreciation at finding someone who wanted to help. The smallest act of kindness was like a drink of water after three days in the desert.

Arriving home I was beginning to hurt, and I felt truly exhausted. I thought about leaving the books in the car, but I desperately needed the information they contained. Slowly, I carried everything in. It took three trips. On the last trip, the phone was ringing. I chose not to answer it until I remembered I had turned the answering machine off earlier. By the time I reached the phone, it had stopped ringing. I thought it might be the hospital and then felt sick. Tearing through the bags on the kitchen table, I was trying to find the number of the hospital. I began throwing things: a stuffed teddy bear, cards, that silly, pink water pitcher and damned water basin. Where in the hell was the sheet with the hospital's number? Finally! There it was. My hand was shaking as I picked up the phone and tried to dial the number. The voice answered, "Nursery."

"Uh, this is Linda Johnson. I'm checking on Jaime."

"She's fine. She just ate and she's sleeping."

"I'll be there for the next feeding."

"That's not necessary. You really need your rest."

"I want to be there," I hung up before the nurse knew I was crying.

I leaned against the wall. The kitchen was a mess with everything that had been thrown from the bags. Tears streamed down my cheeks. I had been holding my emotions in at the hospital. I hadn't wanted anyone to see me cry. They were all so amazed at how well I was handling this situation. The built-up hurt

31

and sorrow came out in one loud wail, "Why?" as I slid down the wall, gripped my stomach, and allowed myself to openly cry with no restraint. My chest heaved and I sobbed and sobbed for a long time, releasing the demons of worry and fear that only the mother of a special needs child would know. After tears stopped I felt empty, desolate. I had no energy to get up. I curled up in a ball and fell asleep on the floor.

When I awoke it was dark outside. Darn! Carl would be home and the place was a disaster. Pulling myself up, I hustled and stuffed as much as I could in the closet in the baby's room. I put the books in there too. I didn't want Carl to know that I had been out against doctor's orders. I just didn't want to talk about it. As I put the books away, I noticed that I had brought *Many Mansions* home. Hmm, I could keep this one out. Since it wasn't one on mental retardation or Down Syndrome he wouldn't know it was a book I just got. It would give me something to read tonight when I got back from the hospital.

The trip back to the hospital was easier and our visit was reassuring. Jaime's color had begun to lighten and she was generally more responsive. They were signs that supported and confirmed my tentative plan to bring her home.

My mother stopped by during the visit and shared that she had received a call from Carl's parents, John and Margaret Johnson. Dr. Hunter had called them to recommend they convince us to place Jaime. Jaime was peaceful and nestled in my arms after eating. The doctor's attempted manipulation to remove her from her rightful place was wrong. Yet this hospital was his kingdom where he was the ruler. As if the nurse could read my mind, she walked up and said, "I need to take her now."

Startled, I pulled Jaime close, heart to heart, cheek to cheek, breathed in the essence of her, kissed her soft cheek, and whispered, "I love you. I'll be back. I promise." Handing her to the nurse always felt like I might never see her again, but my resolve was getting stronger with each passing moment. I was tempted to grab her back and run out of the hospital. I may have actually done it at that moment if I hadn't thought she really needed to be there.

Before leaving, I stopped by Joyce's room to let her know that I had begun our research and had some initial information. She looked rested and at peace. She and her husband had made a decision. They would not need any information on placements. They would be taking their son Tommy home with them. We made plans to get together at her home the following week.

When we left the hospital, Carl said he wanted to stop at his parents. I was sure it was their idea. Especially after knowing they called my mother and attempted to enlist her in their efforts to get me to place Jaime. I insisted we go straight home. I was tired. A visit with them would open up the whole issue of whether or not to keep Jaime. I wasn't in the mood to discuss it. I wanted to be rested when we talked with Carl's parents. It's not that they were ever rude, and I could have handled open discussion. But I knew that would not be the case, so I opted to avoid them for now.

How could I describe my relationship with John and Margaret? It was like an iceberg. Always a little chilly, and much going on that couldn't be seen. The unspoken agreement was to discuss only the surface topics. Trying to talk about Jaime would be almost impossible. I knew they felt the need to protect their son from what they considered to be a lifetime of grief, and the best way to do that would be to place Jaime. They had not even wanted us to have the genetic testing done for fear of the results. When I insisted it be done, they made a comment indicating that if it was hereditary, they expected it would be from my side of the genetic pool.

Just like the genetic testing, everyone seemed to accept whether or not to place Jaime would be my decision. Since it was to be my choice, I decided I would not talk with them until my resolution was final. That way I would not have to listen to subtle suggestions and innuendos about their true feelings. I always found it frustrating that they seemed incapable of being open and forthright. They carefully cloaked all of their mean thoughts in feigned innocence, thinking it served to disguise the ugliness of the true, underlying meaning. It was a ritualistic dance they performed each time there was any major issue that was less than pleasant.

Back at home, the warmth of the tea seeped through the cup into my hands and seemed to flow through my body. Fixing tea was a ritual that connected me to the roots of my British ancestors and to the nurturing received from my grandmother on cold mornings. Grandma Ross would get the coal stove fire roaring and when the tea kettle began singing, it would be warm in the kitchen, and a cup of tea with milk and sugar would be waiting. Grandma kept a blanket near the stove which she would wrap around me as I sat and sipped the morning tea. I had always been close to my grandmother. I wished she were nearby, but she lived in Pennsylvania. Maybe it wouldn't help. This was an odd time and, although loved ones were near, I still felt alone.

I thought about talking with Carl. He was watching TV. But, even when the television wasn't on, there had been an uneasy silence. As much as I needed to connect and be with someone, to feel close to another human being, to feel loved, it hurt to share space with someone. It felt like my skin had turned into a cactus with the outside faced inward and if anyone brushed against me or, God forbid, hugged me, there was the immediate and lasting pain from the contact. So, although I would normally stay up and watch some late night show, tonight, going to bed early seemed to be the best idea. I took *Many Mansions* with me and began to read.

Why had this book been in that section? Why had I noticed it? Why had I taken it off the shelf? Why hadn't it been given to the librarian as planned? I could hardly believe what it was about when I opened it. I remember Vivian saying, "You never know what you'll find in the library." I remembered my cry of "Why?" earlier in the day. After reading only a few pages, I held the book to my breast and gave thanks.

God still seemed to be tuned in to my station and providing answers.

Never before had I thought about or considered such ideas as those contained within this book. Raised Catholic, with the maternal side of the family being Methodist, there were moments while I was reading when I expected the book to burst into flames. I truly had no idea such concepts existed. From an early age I asked questions of the nuns and priests which they found frustrating and troublesome. Questions they couldn't answer, except with their favorite and frequently used response, "Some things we don't understand and you must accept on blind faith." I spent a full year in fifth grade going to church every day and hoping for an answer to a complex question. No such luck. Then in this one small, misplaced book I got a lifetime of questions answered.

Many Mansions was written by Gina Cerminara. She presented her ideas with such clarity and logic that it was difficult to argue with her conclusion. She introduced me to the ideas that the soul is eternal, reincarnation and karma are real, and life is a school. She traced the karmic causes of most diseases and negative conditions, and explained how justice is served through many lifetimes. All of our experiences are grist for the mill of the soul, opportunities for the soul to unfold and discover its true nature.

This was something that made sense to me. If we could only have one life and God is good, then it didn't make any sense to me that some babies would be born with severe handicaps or that children would die young without a chance to live. But, if we could have multiple lives – even if we don't remember them – and we learn from them or others learn from them, that type of logic made sense to me. My faith was renewed.

I just gave birth to a child with Down Syndrome. It meant she would be mentally retarded. Some people seemed to think it was the worst thing that ever happened. Through the concepts in this book I learned it was not something horrible happening to me, but instead, I was being given an opportunity for my soul to unfold, discover new meaning, and to grow. And I have the opportunity to watch this soul, who found her way onto this earth through me, to expand and mature and develop.

I was now excited about our future. There was no longer fear, nor sadness, nor doubt – I was bringing my daughter home – and we had work to do, together.

– II –

Hidden Gifts

Our problems come with gifts in their hands, we need our problems because we need their gifts.

~ Richard Bach, Illusions

Giving and Receiving

Once the decision was made to bring Jaime home, there were no problems. No one challenges a mother lion.

Jaime's tiny face peaked out from the delicate yellow crocheted blanket that wrapped around her as we left the hospital. I chose yellow to express our mood. It represented sunshine and life and our new-found hope. I gave Jaime her name because someone told me it meant sunshine.

When the hospital doors opened and I stepped outside, the fresh spring air swept the path in front of us. Sunlight danced on newly watered grass. I peeked into the blanket and saw Jaime was now rosy cheeked and bright eyed. She was as beautiful as this gorgeous spring day. No, more beautiful. This was an amazingly wonderful baby that I held in my arms as I left the hospital. This was how a new mother should feel.

Even John and Margaret were supportive when they realized I remained standing after many rounds with Dr. Hunter. Out of concern for our welfare and at a loss for knowing what else to do, Margaret called the Public Health Department. Nurse Sandra Jennings was assigned to our case. When she arrived she was visibly upset. Her job was to help families who were in medical need. She honestly did not know what to do for us. It only added to her confusion to find me happy.

Over a cup of tea she expressed relief after I provided information to her about Down Syndrome. She said she hadn't known much about it before, and now felt more prepared for any future cases she might encounter. In turn, she informed me that Margaret's suggestion for me to set an alarm every two hours to wake Jaime for feedings was unnecessary. What a relief. This routine had been carried out faithfully over the past month. It had been exhausting.

With alarms turned off the next night, we slept peacefully. The next morning when I woke up and looked at the clock, my heart leapt into my throat. I had been sleeping eleven hours! Jaime! What happened to Jaime? I jumped out of bed and ran to the bassinette only to find Jaime sound asleep. She must have been more exhausted than I was from the routine! Learning to follow my own instincts and not the well meaning advice of others was a lesson I would have many opportunities to practice.

The first real help was through a county program for infants who were considered to be at risk and needed early intervention. Nancy Springer, early infant specialist, was assigned to our home. She should have arrived in a chariot with trumpets blazing. She had curly blonde hair and enough energy to keep a family warm for a winter. Each week she dragged in her bag of equipment and the toys which she used to encourage Jaime to learn new skills. Nancy would also teach me how to work with Jaime during the week, in-between her visits. At the beginning of each session Jaime and I would be "tested" on what we had accomplished during the week. I never wanted to disappoint Nancy.

During one of Nancy's visits Joyce stopped by with Tommy, not realizing she would be interrupting a session, "Oh, I'm sorry. I didn't know you were here."

Nancy responded, "No problem. We were just about to wrap up. It's so great you two have each other to talk with. I wish some of my other mothers had someone."

That was all Joyce and I needed to hear. We had been waiting for this opportunity. So, I jumped on it, "That's amazing! We've been talking about how to start connecting with other new mothers. Can you help us?"

With a quizzical look she glanced at Joyce, "You're sure you just happened by here and this wasn't planned?"

"No, no."

"No."

Both Joyce and I responded at the same time, each of us worried that Nancy thought we had set this up.

She laughed, "You should see your faces. Okay. I think you two might have a good idea."

"We'll call ourselves Nancy's Brigade. We can share all the information we've gathered about what's available in the community. We can contact the hospitals and doctors' offices. We can even tell new parents how they can find you." I was on a roll.

Joyce joined in, "We can design information packets. No new parent will ever have to feel alone or lost."

"Just promise me you won't call yourselves Nancy's Brigade."

That was never our formal name, but Nancy's Brigade suited us for our shadow identity. The group began with four mothers. Two years later we had nineteen mothers and friends who were actively participating so we formed our own ARC group. That meant we were a local non-profit chapter of the Association for Retarded Citizens. I had the great privilege of being the founding president.

This was the most amazing collection of women. No one would have put us together by choice. The personalities were so strong and so different, if they had been colors, many people would immediately have become violently ill at seeing them all together in one room. But we had a mutual purpose that bridged our differences. To say that I am proud of my affiliation with the women who belonged to that group would be a gross understatement. We laughed, cried, and had intense disagreements. We loved, honored, and appreciated each other's accomplishments. There was tremendous respect for the challenges that each of the mothers faced. We learned about each other's child's disability.

The Brigade focused on advocacy, frequently organizing groups to change the current system or to create new programs. My home turned into a factory each time there was an upcoming function requiring a new project. Multiple playpens and several sewing machines were part of my eclectic décor.

Fund raising is always a challenge for any nonprofit group; ours was no exception. We were mostly young and full of enthusiasm and tired of bake sales. The city-wide bazaar was created from boredom.

It began when Janet shared, "I'm quitting if I have to bake another cookie."

"Then why don't you come up with a better idea to make some real money?" Shirley goaded her, "Your cookies aren't that great anyway." Janet made a face at her.

Karen said, "Hey, that's a great idea. Let's do something city-wide, like a big garage sale and charge everyone for their space."

Mary, who never liked anything, didn't disappoint us when she commented, "That will never work."

Her negativity was often a catalyst for the group. Several women chimed in with opposite views. Before the night ended, we decided to offer the other twenty-eight ARCs in the area the opportunity to participate in a city-wide bazaar. My commitment was to find a place, arrange for set-up, contact radio and TV stations, and invite directors of the special education programs as well as the mayor. After they left I wondered what in the world I had gotten myself into this time. Much to my surprise it was a huge success. A nightmare to organize, but we had fun, made some decent money, and our programs now had better financial backing.

Joyce and I continued to focus on the Parent to Parent program. We prepared information packets and delivered them to doctors' offices and hospital nurseries. It was before the age of computers, so they weren't as professional as we would have liked. We worked within our group to develop a comprehensive training program for approaching new parents, recognizing there are many different feelings and ways of handling this sensitive situation. We felt prepared, but were disappointed. We received very few calls. Mostly referrals came by word of mouth, through a friend or family member, or through someone who knew someone who knew one of us. The doctors and hospitals would not work with individuals. We needed a larger, established organization.

Other women in the ARC had their pet projects. Shirley sponsored a Public Speaking and Advocacy program for providing information to the community. Her favorite targets were school systems. She wanted to educate students, to teach them about developmental disabilities and mental retardation. Most school systems wanted to know what organization backed her and were not satisfied with her just being from an ARC. She wanted, actually needed, handouts, and those would be costly.

The third big project born from our group was huge. Several mothers led by Diane had children with severe multiple disabilities and required constant monitoring. These mothers had trouble finding anyone to care for their children. They couldn't go on simple errands during the day, such as the grocery or drug store, or to tend to their own self-care, like going to a beauty shop or a doctor's office. The biggest need in their lives was to have a place where they could leave their child for a few hours, knowing their child would be safe. They needed respite care. There was nothing available. They created an exchange between themselves, but they needed a professional center. They found a great house and a grant that was a possibility. None of us knew anything about writing grants, nor did we want to get into running a business like a respite center. This would require a real organization.

The county had the Council for Retarded Citizens (CRC), a professional group with a board of directors. They knew about grant writing and ran several programs for developmental disabilities in the area. We met with the director and shared what we had already accomplished with each of the programs. CRC adopted each of the ARC's programs and found federal funding for all of them. They developed and grew them into fully Technicolor visions we had only dreamed about a few short years before.

My desire to make the world a better place extended beyond the ARC which Joyce and I started, and soon expanded to include involvement at county, state, and national levels. In the financial world, when someone gives out more than they receive, they get relatively quick negative feedback. That is not so true in the emotional and mental worlds; the checks and balances system for our general well-being seems to run on a totally different system. It was a time when I was fueled by activity. More days than not, I was only getting four or five hours sleep so I could meet all of my commitments. The world needed me. I had become an organizational addict. I was in love with life and considered myself to be one of the luckiest people on earth.

Moving On

Some days were easier than others and I don't want to give the impression that there were no difficult moments, because there were. I remember a time right after Jaime came home when the envelope came from Children's Hospital with the genetic testing results. I wasn't ready to deal with it, so I placed it on the shelf and ignored it. I tried not to walk into the living-room, knowing it was in there, but the ignoring thing did not work well. The entire afternoon my chest felt like my heart had turned to steel and that envelope was like a giant magnet.

My thoughts wouldn't leave me alone. Open it before Carl gets home, that way if it's bad you don't have to tell him... he never asks anyway... don't open it... put it in a book and forget that it came... you don't want any more children anyway... this has been too hard.

So, if it's been too hard, why not open it?

At one point, I walked in, picked up the envelope, and took it to the kitchen table where all the important events of life seem to happen in our family. I held it for a long time. Then I returned it to the book shelf, this time placing it between two books. This process went on for two days.

The calendar seemed to speak as I walked by, "Friday." I knew the weekend loomed ahead in an unforgiving pattern, Carl would be home, friends would stop by, and there would be little to no chance of being alone. If it was bad news, I wanted to be alone. I quickly walked into the living-room and grabbed the letter. With stabbing gestures I ripped at the flap. The envelope dropped to the floor as I held on to the papers that had pages of strange squiggles and diagrams. The first page was the important one and the words stood out...Trisomy-21. I had studied enough to know what that meant. Jaime's Down Syndrome was not hereditary. My heart raced, chin quivered, and legs gave out as I crumpled onto the floor. Quietly I gasped for air. I held the papers to my heart. "Yes... yes... yes!"

Neither Carl nor I would have to hold any blame or shame. Why would it have had to be that way? Why would one of us have had to bear the guilt? I didn't understand, but I knew it as the reality of what would have been if the results of the test had been different. I was so thankful we wouldn't have to go through that.

My heart then hurt for every parent who received a letter like this that did not have good news. Strange, a year ago I knew absolutely nothing about Down Syndrome or mental retardation and now the most personal news connected me to the thousands of unseen faces of all the families with children with disabilities. In a strange way I felt closer to strangers I never met than to people I knew from the community, and even to many in members of my family. A bond exists which cannot be easily explained or understood.

So, while I was there on the floor, it seemed a good time to offer a prayer of thanks, and add a prayer of protection for all the children and parents who might need a little help. I once heard that every time you sent out a loving thought to someone, it was like sending an angel. It always made me smile to think of being an angel dispatcher. It seemed like I could have spent days in prayer, just sending angels out to all the families with children who have disabilities, but I had to return to the physical realm.

As much as I enjoyed praying, I enjoyed working in the "real world." My life was no longer my own. Jaime required hours of attention with her early infant stimulation exercises. The involvement in ARC activities had begun to increase. Carl was working longer hours. Quiet time was the exception, an anomaly; prayers were said on the run.

Jaime's birth turned our world upside down and changed our life completely. The early trauma was created primarily from misinformation and mishandling by Dr. Hunter. His general ineptness had taken its toll. The other amazing events that surrounded Jaime's birth left me in awe of the entire situation: having a geneticist in the next hospital bed, the surprise of another baby with Down Syndrome born the next day at the same hospital, and the misfiled book *Many Mansions*. All of this came together with other minor events as if watching the creation of a major Broadway production – I, the supporting actress, and Jaime, the star. I was still trying to catch my breath.

Little did I know the pace of life would pick up even more and the genetic information would be almost a necessity to soothe my heart and mind. Neither Carl nor I discussed having another child. So the unexpected arrival of our son, Jay, eighteen months after Jaime proved that the best events in life are unplanned.

Many people asked if I worried while carrying Jay. The genetic testing soothed my mind. There was no concern about having a baby with Down Syndrome. However, I now had many friends who were mothers of children with numerous different types of disabilities. Thinking about some of the possibilities left few nights with restful sleep. I wondered about the future with my unborn child far more than I ever did while carrying Jaime. I also knew after the past year and a half, we would be okay. I now had a support system and knew where and how to get help. I wouldn't be lost like the last time. My prayers for a healthy baby were answered. Jay was not only a handsome baby, he had no disability.

Two children could not be more different. From the beginning Jaime was female, blonde, blue/hazel eyes, tranquil, laid-back, and quiet. Jay was male, black hair, brown eyes, energetic, swift, and boisterous. Being only eighteen months apart, in their early years they acted like twins. They were inseparable. His activity level began to energize her. They exhausted me.

If I allowed them to take a nap during the day they were up at night, and that proved to be dangerous. For example, once I found them playing pirates with my butcher knives. Another time they climbed up to the top of the refrigerator to get two bottles of Flintstone vitamins with iron, and ate the entire contents of both bottles. The doctor said they will most likely never need iron supplements again. Keeping ahead of them was a constant struggle.

Jay, eventually, began to pass Jaime in skills and wanted to do more activities with his peers. Jaime was normally included in the neighborhood play groups and Jay was always protective. But once in a while, he would put his foot down and demand alone time with his friends. I supported his independence and encouraged Jaime to entertain herself in some other way. These events did not go unnoticed by Jaime. I remember one particular time when Jaime was left out of her brother's activities. The next day she insisted on fixing his lunch for school. I should have been more observant. But by the age of nine, Jaime was fairly proficient in the kitchen.

The next day Jay came home from school screaming, "I'm going to kill her!"

Shocked to hear him say something like that about Jaime, I grabbed him before he could go any further, "Whoa! What is going on?"

He had tears in his eyes. I held him close and comforted him, "Oh, honey, what in the world happened?"

I felt him shaking. I watched him and continued to hold him. Then a strange thing happened, he started laughing. He was still crying, but he was also laughing, "She...she...she put dog food in my sandwich. She was mad at me. She made me a dog food sandwich!"

"Oh, Jay, I can't believe she would do that. Not on purpose."

Jaime must have been eavesdropping for she came around the corner – smiling and proud of herself – wanting to accept the responsibility, "Yes...yes, I did."

We had a long talk. As her consequence, Jaime did Jay's chores for two weeks. She didn't seem to mind. To this day they laugh about it. She still doesn't like to be left out of things and she will let people know it, but she hasn't made anyone dog food sandwiches – only her brother, that one time.

Hard Times

A research study on families with special needs children reported that those parents are twice as likely to get divorced as other people. When I read the research results, it never occurred to me that we would be one of those families. But we were. An interesting thing about separations and divorces – rarely do the two people involved have the same perceptions. Each of us has a different version of our story. I can only share mine. So when Carl said he didn't love me anymore, that he'd never loved me, it hurt. After that, we stopped being together. For the sake of the children we continued to live in the same house.

When things got too painful, the children and I would spend time with distant relatives, only to return within a few days or weeks. This pattern was repeated until we both admitted staying together wasn't working. We attempted a friendly divorce, but that didn't work either. I cried a lot. Jaime was seven years old and didn't understand why Mommy was sad and Daddy didn't come home anymore. Jay wanted to know why we were getting a "diborce." It was an ugly, unhappy time. We managed to get through it by living life day by day.

I continued as much involvement as possible with my volunteer work, attempting to appear unconcerned and quite unaffected by the entire process. It didn't work very well. Life became strange and stressful. I didn't feel like offering explanations. People are naturally curious and generally unforgiving when someone doesn't meet their expectations. Some of my best friends and consistent supporters distanced themselves.

I was forced to start a new chapter in my life. It seemed like an entirely different book, but it was actually just a new release within a series. Many of the characters were the same and yet life was different. My father received a promotion and my parents moved to another state. Now with Carl gone, I was really alone. Carl made it painfully clear that neither he nor his family would be my babysitters. There was no option about working, we needed money to survive. I had no choice but to withdraw from activities. The majority of my energy was spent on working and keeping a home for my two children.

The divorce was finalized in November. It was the week before Thanksgiving. The children would be going with Carl to his parent's. I would be spending the day alone. I decided to hate the holidays, which had always been a favorite time of year for me. The idea of celebrating Christmas was too painful and exhausting to consider. In the midst of gloomy daydreaming about how to avoid the upcoming season, the doorbell rang. When I opened it a pretty blonde bounced into the house like an errant ball. Her speech matched her body movements, "Hi, I'm Carol from next door, Shelly's mom. We haven't met yet, but I thought it was time. Shelly baby-sits for you and we're both single moms now. I know your name is Linda. You weren't busy were you? I didn't see any cars outside or anything." She finally stopped to take a breath.

I just looked at her, not sure what to say, "Uh, yeah, my name is Linda. And Shelly sits for my kids."

Carol looked at me and began laughing. "Oops, looks like I've done it again, just barged right in...overdrive...sorry. Shelly told me about your divorce, and Carl moving out. I thought you could use a friend. I've been doing this single thing for a long time; I know the holidays are tough, so I thought I'd simply dive in. I really am sorry if I came on too strong."

I laughed. There was something about her that I liked – a lot. "Why don't you come in and have some coffee, or would you prefer tea?"

"How about a Bloody Mary? It's Sunday and I like a brunch drink." She then reached into her oversized purse and pulled out all the ingredients. "Do you have a glass?"

I pulled glasses out of the cupboard. Carol made the drinks and we toasted our new friendship. This was a most unusual person who had just entered my life. Chances are I would like her. The events that followed set a pattern that lasted a lifetime.

Carol looked around the house and asked, "When are you going to start decorating for Christmas?"

"Truthfully, I was thinking about it right before you came over. I don't feel much like Christmas this year. I may not decorate."

Carol's eyes got big, like the children in the Keene pictures. "What? No! I will not hear that." Her hands flew to cover her ears. "You don't have a choice. Christmas isn't about you. Christmas isn't about how you feel. You decided to get a divorce. That was your decision. You're an adult, you can do that. You have two children. There are things you have to do that you don't want to. They didn't ask you to get a divorce. Christmas is about them. You have a responsibility to them. Just because you feel sad doesn't mean you give up your responsibility. No sir! You will decorate this house. You will celebrate Christmas...because Christmas is about the kids, not you!"

She was finally silent. She locked eyes with me. I was in awe. I hadn't seen anyone show that much passion in a long time. In fact, Carol reminded me of myself when I got excited about something. She almost made me want to feel the spirit of Christmas again. The kids deserved that.

Tears filled my eyes, "Thanks, Carol. I needed the wake up call. Now I just hope I can find the energy to pull it off."

She rolled her eyes. "Okay, this is how you do it. You set a tradition and you never, and I mean never, vary from it."

I gave her a quizzical look.

She smiled and said, "Do you want me to do all the work?"

I nodded my head.

She laughed, "Okay, but then you're going to be stuck with it. We'll start you off this first year. The day after Thanksgiving will be the day you decorate your home for Christmas. Get your stuff out and we'll be here about noon. Plan a casual dinner. We'll have fun."

Carol, Shelly, and my children decorated our home, put the Christmas tree up, and baked some cookies. We had a festive casual dinner. It was a marvelous day. She helped our family begin a new tradition. That tradition remains the same thirty years later, for me, and for Jay and his family. In my heart the day after Thanksgiving will always be "Carol Day." God was continuing to send his messengers just when I needed them. We were fortunate to have new friends enter our lives, always at the right time.

Wedding bells tolled for Carl five months after our divorce. This was a first marriage for his new wife, Martha. She was overwhelmed by Jaime and Jay's youthful exuberance. The every other weekend visits became increasingly rare, until months went by without a Daddy sighting. Any suggestion about the children missing him was met with a reminder that he was not my babysitter. I made excuses to Jaime and Jay that Daddy was busy.

Months crept by, and each seemed to hold a special challenge. A business associate introduced me to his sister, Kathey. She was a single woman who enjoyed the children. Our friendship blossomed quickly and within two months we had discussed the idea of her moving in with us. After some negotiations and agreements, Kathey became part of our family. With another adult helping, life became manageable. I could work and take care of household duties and had energy left to tend to the children's needs and activities.

When the second Christmas rolled around, the children received invitations to join Carl and Martha for family festivities. I was happy Jaime and Jay were excited to spend time with their father and paternal grandparents, but the idea of being without the children for Christmas caused a deep sense of holiday blues. Kathey had no plans, as her brother was returning to Alabama to be with family. On Christmas Eve we chose some records by The Mormon Tabernacle Choir, Barbara Streisand, and Perry Como, and listened to favorite seasonal sounds as we reminisced about previous holidays.

In the middle of sharing a story, the tune White Christmas began playing and Kathey started crying, "This is the first time I'm not going to be with my family on Christmas."

No one should cry alone, so I joined her. After a few minutes of silent tears I commented, "I wonder how many other people are feeling like us right now?"

"Well, I know that Barb and Karen are by themselves."

"Carol's kids left with their dad, so she's alone. We should ask her over. We should invite all of them."

"What? Tonight?" She looked around the living-room which needed cleaning.

"No, but we can start calling people now and invite them for tomorrow."

"We don't have enough food. We can't get ready that fast to do a formal dinner."

"So what, remember the loaves and the fishes? We'll ask everyone to bring something. You're thinking old traditions. I want to start some new ones. It won't be formal. Let's make a casual Holiday Open House party. I'll barbecue a ham for sandwiches, get some buns, and make a veggie plate."

As our enthusiasm grew, Kathey and I thought of other people who might be alone. Our first call was to Carol. She said she had already made plans, a friend was coming over to spend the day with her. "So? Why don't you bring him over?"

"What a great idea! I wasn't sure what we were going to do for the entire day. I just didn't want to be alone."

"We feel the same way. No one should be alone on Christmas. If you think of others who may be, invite them."

Each call generated more guests, totaling twenty-three people who would not have to spend Christmas Day alone. It was an amazing time, including the opportunity to make new friends. Several musicians brought instruments and entertained. We set out jigsaw puzzles and chess and backgammon boards. Everyone relaxed and enjoyed the evening. The spirit of the season embraced all of us. New arrivals were greeted with a round of "We wish you a Merry Christmas." The house exuded warmth and joy. It was a huge success.

When the children returned in the late afternoon, they were surprised to find a party. Jaime's response, "Why you not wait me?" spoke volumes. Jaime used shorthand speech, but her message was clear, she was disappointed she missed part of a "fun day."

"We wanted to surprise you."

"Oh... " She pondered the answer, and then smiled, "I be happy."

For many years we kept the Open House tradition. It got bigger every year making our little home bulge with Christmas spirit. The children didn't want to miss out on any of the fun and at times refused to go with their dad. After some discussion, we developed a plan. They spent Christmas Eve and part of the next day with their father and returned home in the early afternoon. We never spent Christmas alone.

After the year of adjustment to being divorced, life slowly improved. I worked my way into a management position with a well-known and respected independent telephone company. A major achievement, considering my formal education ended with high school. Knowing any further advancement would require additional education, I enrolled in business courses at an excellent private school, Capital University.

Finding time to study was difficult. I decided the only thing I could do was to sleep less. After six weeks of only two or three hours of sleep a night I was rushed to the hospital. The doctors were unable to diagnose my condition. It took a week before I was stable. Two more emergency runs and hospital stays took place before a doctor asked the right questions and diagnosed me with "Marathon Syndrome." Not an official diagnosis, but it happens when a person depletes their body's resources. The only way back to health was time and rest.

Kathey worked during the day and I couldn't find anyone to help with the children. I called Carl. He agreed to help. They stayed with him for the full two weeks while I was recovering. They had never stayed away for more than a night; it was a long two weeks. Seeing them run up to the house on the day they returned, my heart filled with joy. I loved my children. They were so beautiful. During the two weeks of recovery I made some decisions about priorities. The children were number one and my education would have to wait.

Carl stepped inside the door and announced, "I'll be picking Jay up this weekend. We made plans."

I was so grateful that they helped out while I was sick, I decided not to object or remind him that his visitation was only every other weekend. Then I thought about what he said and asked, "What about Jaime?"

"Uh, she won't feel comfortable with what we're doing."

"Exactly what are you doing?"

"Linda, there is nothing in any agreement that says I have to tell you what we do. Listen, we just did you a big favor taking care of the kids. We didn't have to do that. I'm going to pick up Jay Saturday – or, I can just keep him. That might be better." He then shouted, "Hey, Jay, get your bag, you're goin' back with me." With that he turned and walked out of the house.

Waves of hurt and anger surged through me, each vying for attention. While I was trying to act calm Jay ran out to the living room with an excited grin, "Thanks, Mom." He gave me a quick kiss before grabbing his bag and rushing out the door.

Jaime picked up her bag and looked at me, unsure of what to do. Her name had not been called. The look on her face expressed utter confusion. To see her standing at the door as they drove away broke my heart, a common mother's wound.

After that there were many weekends when Jay went with his Dad and Jaime was left behind. We would do special things on those weekends. I called them ladies' days, fun days, or any other term I could think of, to make it appear as my idea for her to remain with me. I did not want her to feel left out.

When Jay returned from one of his weekends, he asked to talk. Seated at the table, his large brown eyes seemed to wish for the wisdom of a sage. He began, "Mom, I don't want to hurt you." This was a sure signal whatever was coming next was going to be extremely painful. He stopped for a moment before going on, "but I want to go live with Dad and Martha."

Deep breath...my world began to swirl. Not since the news of being told that I had a "bad baby" had I felt like this. This time it was my child delivering the news. It was not fair. Carl shouldn't have asked Jay to do this. He was too cowardly to do it himself, to tell me he convinced our son to leave his mother. So, he sent a child to do it? I took another deep breath. Jay continued to look at me, his eyes filled with tears.

I wanted to tell him it would be okay, although it wasn't But I did anyway, "It's okay, Jay. Don't cry. We'll figure this out. Have you talked with your dad about this?" I knew he had. Jay nodded. "Can you tell me some of your thoughts about it?"

Using his hand to wipe his face "Well"... sigh... "Martha doesn't work so she has lots more time to spend with me. She can help me with my homework and take me places. Dad said he will get a dirt bike for me and we can ride together. They are going on vacation to Florida – Disneyland – and Denver next year. I could go with them. And, they talked about how hard it is with you and Jaime...and...well...and I wouldn't have to always be around Jaime and stuff...and have other people see me with her and ...." then he started really crying. I held him. Then we talked and talked about reasons to go or not to go. The promises to fulfill a ten year-old's dreams won the tug of war going on in his heart. Within the month he packed his bags and moved to his dad's.

Often I wondered how this could have happened. Had I been out of touch with Jay's needs? Something always seemed to be happening with Jaime and the other special needs projects that made it necessary for me to be out "slaying dragons." But I never ignored Jay; I tried to stay aware of his needs and make sure he was involved in activities, surrounded with friends, and given a sufficient opportunity to experience enough of life's wonders so he would not resent his sister. But these were hard times.

— III —

An Education

A good education is the next best thing to a pushy mother.
~ Charles Schulz

Student and Teacher

One of the many dragons Jaime and I occasionally faced was the educational system. Her story would be incomplete without sharing some of the educational escapades. Accessing services, especially from the school systems, was a learning experience in advocacy.

When Jaime began attending school her world opened up. This singular event brought a plethora of people and new experiences into our lives. I began to fully appreciate Eleanor Roosevelt's statement, "All of life is a constant education."

From the time of her birth, Jaime was my teacher. Her courses included such basic subjects as tenacity, kindness, tolerance, forgiveness, and authenticity, the ability to be truly genuine and without guile. Her instruction was laced with humor and her tests were always about love.

Many parents blazed the path of special education before the 1970's, which made it possible for Jaime to attend a special preschool. Miss Saunders greeted us with an open smile. Jaime arrived in a virtual heaven to find several playmates and a room filled with toys. She immediately began her exploration. Miss Saunders urged all the parents to leave so she could begin her class.

Each day when I picked Jaime up, she ran to greet me, enthusiastic and giggling. She loved school and everything seemed to be going well – until the parent-teacher conference.

The first words from Miss Saunders put me on notice; this was not going to be a happy occasion. "Jaime is overly active and it is difficult to get her to focus." The look on my face must have made her reconsider her approach, "Don't get me wrong, I like Jaime. She just isn't meeting her goal."

I cleared my throat before responding, "Exactly what is her goal?"

"Well, I want her to be able to sit still for fifteen minutes, with her hands folded in her lap."

Now I was chewing on my lower lip, a bad habit and a sure indication I was getting upset. "Do you have anything else to report? What has she learned since she started?"

Miss Saunders didn't know me very well, but she knew this meeting was not going as she had planned, "My primary focus has been to get her to settle down. Until she can do that, I really am not able to do much with her."

"So, how many minutes is she up to?"

"Well, some days are better than others. Her longest time has been ten minutes. Most of the time, she only manages five."

"Hmm...How many times does she practice this each day?"

"I set a timer for every fifteen minutes, and then she sits in the chair."

"I'm having a hard time with this. I expected more of the program."

She wasn't about to back down, "I know it may seem disappointing, but each child's program is geared to what they need to learn and this is what she needs."

Disappointment was an understatement. To have a single educational goal for a five year old developmentally disabled child to sit still was incomprehensible.

Fury fueled my actions. Immediately upon arriving home, I called the county school program and began my education about how to advocate for my child. Lesson One: Only talk to someone who can do something about the situation. Within three phone calls I was talking to Dr. Porter, the director of special education. Late afternoon I received a call from Miss Saunders stating Jaime would have new goals. By the end of the school year Jaime was expected to count to ten and be able to identify ten words.

I decided to be a frequent, unexpected visitor in the classroom, as were Miss Saunders' supervisor and the director. Jaime achieved her goals by February, allowing us to establish more challenging goals. It didn't surprise me to learn when the school began to focus on helping Jaime to learn something useful, her behavior improved dramatically. At the end of the year in the midst of our farewells and summarizing Jaime's accomplishments, Miss Saunders said an interesting thing, "I've learned a lot this year from my students and parents." She paused and smiled before saying, "I learned the squeaky wheel gets oiled, but no one knows that better than you." I nodded in agreement. It was part of my education. I passed that test and the lesson has stayed with me. I don't think Miss Saunders realized the impact of her closing sentiments. They were like encouraging words at a graduation ceremony.

Transportation

The next year was another big step – bus transportation. I prepared Jaime with stories and songs about buses. She was excited. I was nervous. The bus appeared right on schedule. Karen, the bus driver, called Jaime by name as she open the bus door. Her friendly welcome calmed my fears. I helped Jaime up the steps and into the seat. Looking around I asked, "Where's the safety belt?"

"We don't have any."

"What?"

"We've asked for them for a long time, but they keep making excuses. Don't worry, I'll keep my eye on her and be really careful."

The thought crossed my mind not to allow her to go, but she was on the bus and really looking forward to this day. The schools had been transporting kids for years. I decided I would let her go today, but something had to be done. I initiated the first step in advocacy: call someone who can do something about the situation. No seat belts on a school bus seemed to be a problem for the director. So I placed a call, "Is Dr. Porter in? This is Linda Johnson."

After a couple of moments he answered, "Well, Linda, to what do I owe this unexpected pleasure?"

"You know I don't bother you unless it's important."

He laughed, "That's one of the things I love about you, right to the point. So, how can I help? Can't be another teacher issue, the kids aren't in the classrooms yet."

"Jaime is being transported on the bus this year and when it arrived there were no seatbelts. Dr. Porter, this is a big problem when driving around with someone like Jaime on the bus. I don't think you want to have that kind of responsibility hanging over your head. One accident could ruin the entire program. Can you imagine what the lawyers would do if they got involved? I'm sure you didn't know about the buses not having seatbelts. And, I'm sure you don't want the media to know about it either."

At first there was silence, and then he chuckled, "You certainly do have a way with words, Linda. No, I didn't know about this and, yes, I do think we can do something about it. You have a right to be concerned. Give me a chance to work on this before you start calling in the cavalry."

"As I said earlier, I don't like to bother you or hassle you with calls, so when should I expect to hear something?"

"I'll get back within the next three days, will that be good enough?"

"Thank you. I really mean it. This is about the kids' safety."

"I agree."

The bus returned at one o'clock. Karen's face reminded me of a child's on Christmas morning when they've just received their first bicycle. She could barely speak, "Who *are* you?"

Confused, I shrugged my shoulders and said, "Linda Johnson, why?"

She got up, motioned me onto the bus and said, "Look,... look... we have seat belts."

I don't know how they did it. They must have had the seat belts and just didn't install them until I called. I'm sure Jaime's bus was the first bus they put them in.

I laughed. My friends from the library shelves really helped me with this one. I'd read several books on how to get what you needed: Nurture relationships at all levels; talk with the person who can actually do what you need to have done; tell them clearly what the problem is; give them a solution; outline the consequences if no action is taken; set a time line; and always be pleasant. It was a formula for success that I would use many times over the years when advocating for a cause. Without the inspiration of Jaime's needs, I doubt I would have developed this skill.

IQ Tests

Learning to navigate the school systems often seemed more challenging than manipulating a raft through the roughest rapid whitewaters. As Jaime prepared to move from special education preschool to the public school system, the school psychologists took an interest in her. They began testing to determine the least restrictive program. A mystery began to develop. Within a six month period, Jaime's IQ scores ranged from 48, indicating she was severely mentally retarded, to 71, indicating she was not mentally retarded. I began researching everything I could get my hands on about IQ testing.

The next meeting with the school officials, I requested all the school psychologists be present who had performed testing on Jaime. Within minutes after the meeting started I had asked questions about where, when, and how each of the tests were given. They became quite uncomfortable and one of the school psychologists visibly bristled when it was determined he gave an inappropriate test; another turned red when questioned about an improper procedure. He challenged me, "Who do you think you are and what gives you the right to question us?"

"I'm just a mother, trying to find out how in the world my daughter can be tested and found to be an idiot one month and several months later not even be retarded. I didn't go to college, but I can read and believe it or not there is a library and books available to tell people about IQ tests. I read enough to know you all did not do a very good job. I want her tested again and since she has problems with her speech, I want her to be given the Lieter IQ test. If that's a problem, we can all go to the school board." Looking at the principal I asked, "Is it going to be a problem?"

"No, Linda. Your request sounds reasonable." The advocacy formula worked again.

The school hired an outside psychologist to come to our home and complete the testing. Jaime scored 68, which meant she could go to county schools or public schools. It was my decision. Not an easy decision. The public school's learning handicap class would provide an academic curriculum and increase her opportunities for socialization with the children in regular classes. County Education classes were designed for the more severely handicapped population. Their curriculum was primarily aimed at daily living skills and academics would be secondary.

I considered Jaime's strengths and weaknesses and what I wanted for her life. Jaime received socialization in the neighborhood. School might be a good place to meet people, but regular education students could be vicious. Jaime didn't deal well with cruelty. She flowered when she had the chance to be a star, which she would be in the county program. Basic reading, writing, and math skills were important, but after that, my primary concern would be for her to know how to take care of herself. After visiting both programs, the special education classroom in the county program won my vote. I watched the teacher, Lynn Needle, interacting with each child, meeting them at their individual levels. And best of all, she wasn't afraid to laugh. I knew Jaime would be happy and do well in this class.

Performance

Placing Jaime into Miss Needle's class was definitely the right move. She blossomed.   Miss Needle often called to report Jaime's most recent antics, which she rated from amusing to hilarious.

Jaime loved to see people smile and she entertained herself as she engaged her audience. She was a keen observer and one of her favorite pastimes was imitating what she saw. Her imitations could be from real life, television, or a combination. If you had a bad habit, Jaime would practice it in private until it was perfected and then share it with the first group she encountered. Her favorite was performing 'organ' recitals – burping, passing gas, and blowing her nose. All of these could be done individually or in unison and at will. And, when she completed her performance she would end with a loud effusive, "Ex-c-u-u-se me!" If no one was laughing, she enjoyed getting them started by giggling until she snorted. Part of Jaime's education was learning different ways to be entertaining. Lynn Needles found the right balance not to break Jaime's spirit, but to reduce and finally eliminate organ recitals.

Jaime was a born actress, always on stage, whether at home or in school. Especially school because it offered a larger and more appreciative audience. Trying to share the concept of privacy with someone who is young and mentally delayed is like telling your nose not to run when you have a serious head cold. If you don't want others to see your nose running you stay home or carry a lot of tissues and try to act as if everything is normal. Every time Jaime shared some personal matter, it offered another opportunity for me to learn how to handle embarrassing situations. I knew I had a choice, I could spend much time red-faced, upset, and angry at someone who was doing what came naturally to her, or I could learn to appreciate her talent to imitate and not take life too seriously. I learned to laugh, especially at myself and my bad habits.

As part of her love for imitating and acting, Jaime dressed the part of anyone who captured her interest. Some of her roles were obvious ones, which most children adopt: policeman, fireman, nurse, cowboy, and Indian. If I stopped her from wearing an outfit, she would somehow manage to smuggle it to school within a day or two. She had a variety of ways of sneaking things out of the house, including wearing layered clothing, stashing small items in her back pack and hiding bags with her stash behind bushes so she could grab them on the way to the bus.

Television fascinated Jaime and her favorite program of the year was the Emmy Awards. She loved to watch the actresses and to imitate them, both their actions and their dress. After the Emmys she gathered a wardrobe for her debut at school. She did not share it with me. She must have known this was one of the outfits she would not be permitted to wear out of the house. I had no idea what she was doing until Miss Needle called, "Hey, Linda, I'm not sure who came to school today, but we have a clothing problem."

I was confused. Jaime left wearing jeans with a yellow t-shirt, so that couldn't be it. She must have pulled one of her switches. Miss Needle and I had previously figured it out. She would actually redress herself on the bus or go to the bathroom at school before going to class.

I asked, "Do I want to hear this?"

Lynn chuckled, "Probably not, but I have to tell you. I can't figure this one out. She has a big floppy hat, sun glasses, lots of lipstick, and several necklaces, which is good because they are covering what the blouse doesn't. This must be your blouse. Very sexy – low cut. Probably not as low cut on you, but very low cut on Jaime. Long skirt. You must be missing most of your jewelry box. She has rings on every finger and bracelets up both arms. She's also wearing a shawl. But I have to tell you the part I like best is the pink gloves. She has long pink gloves which go all the way up her arms. They must be elbow length, but for her they go all the way." She laughed, "This is the crowning jewel of her outfits. Who is she supposed to be?"

I held my head while Lynn described each detail of Jaime's current costume. In a flash I saw Jaime's bright eyes watching the awards. "Uh, I think you actually have Jaime. She's ready to receive her Emmy."

Lynn got it immediately, "Should I?"

"If you do, I will personally report you to the school board. Do not encourage her. I am sure by your description she has gotten enough attention already. Make her take it off. She has blue jeans and a yellow t-shirt with her."

"You're no fun."

"I know. It's part of the mother routine."

We then talked seriously and developed a behavior plan for addressing Jaime's costumes, without killing her spirit or creativity.

Show and Tell

Show and tell time was part of every school day. Jaime always scouted the house for something interesting, different, and unusual to share. She did not always share with me what she shared with the class. Actually, the more "interesting" objects that she took to school were often purposefully secreted in her book bag to get by her mother's inquisitive eyes.

I knew it was Lynn Needle laughing when I picked up the phone. Each time she began to speak, she would start laughing again. She couldn't seem to stop. It was the end of the day, after the children were on the bus. I began to worry. She was absolutely hysterical. Finally she calmed down sufficiently to take several deep breaths and said, "Oh my God, Linda, you won't believe what she did today." This did not make me feel warm and fuzzy, but I tried to stay calm; after all, she was laughing. The words finally spilled out of her, "We had show and tell. You know how much she likes show and tell." She chuckled. "Linda, I just love her new bra!" Now she howled with laughter.

The picture of Jaime sitting with all the little girls and boys in the show and tell circle and waiting for her turn flashed in my mind's eye. I could see her lifting her blouse to proudly display her brand new bra. It was just too much. I groaned, which made

Lynn laugh even more. "Oh, I wish you had been here."

"I'm quite glad I wasn't. Did you explain that show and tell was not the right arena to share her new bra? That it isn't appropriate to take your clothes off at school?"

"Yeah, yeah, of course we did all that stuff. I thought you would find it funny or I wouldn't have even told you."

"Sometimes I just worry about her – and what you may be deciding not to tell me."

"Good, it's your job to worry. I gotta go." Lynn was never one for long drawn out conversations. If she thought I was being too serious, she would just ignore me. She provided the perfect counterbalance to keep parental perspectives from getting completely out of control.

Parent Night

Every year Jaime's school combined parent-night with a short presentation by each class. Needless to say, Jaime was ecstatic at the prospect of being on stage. To have a room full of people who were there to see her thrilled her beyond words. Explaining to her that there were six other classes performing and the people were there to see their children, didn't seem to faze her. This was her opportunity to be on stage and be a star.

For most children, waiting for the curtain to rise was excruciating. You could see the look of terror when the curtain rose and they saw an auditorium filled with grown-ups gawking at them. For many children performing on stage was nearly unbearable. Not Jaime. She could hardly wait for her class to have their time on the stage. Jaime impatiently squirmed in her seat while the other classes presented short essays and songs. Her class was the last to present.

Miss Needle was busy organizing children behind the closed curtain when it parted slightly. A head jutted out and then quickly disappeared. The audience snickered. In response to the audience approval, the head returned, this time with a big smile and now part of a shoulder, and then back behind the curtain again. The audience laughed loudly. I groaned silently and covered my face. This was Jaime's stage debut and she had captured the attention of the audience. I knew before it happened her two head shots were not going to appease the pent up actress within her. She did not disappoint me.

Out she came, pushing the curtain behind her and moving so she was away from the center. She knew it would not be long before Miss Needle would be curious about the laughter and be trying to end her solo career. It was her big chance. She took full advantage of it. She curtsied before she began dancing. The audience clapped. Now Miss Needle's hand was reaching around the curtain to rein in her wayward, overzealous starlet. This brought increasing joy from the audience and greater than ever enthusiasm from Jaime.

Miss Needle finally decided to stop fighting the situation and realized there was no hope in her ability to remain the anonymous arm that captured the jubilant dancer. She stepped out from behind the curtain, waved her arm in Jaime's direction and said, "This is Jaime Johnson, our ice-breaker, the opening act for Room 12." The audience applauded wildly. Jaime was finally satisfied. She bowed and followed Miss Needle back through the closed curtain. I slipped down in my chair and was pleased no one recognized me as the starlet's mother.

Jaime thoroughly enjoyed her second debut almost as much as her first. For the past two weeks she had spent many hours practicing Old McDonald and Happy Days. No amount of practice would make perfect her low-pitched, out-of-tune singing voice. However, what she lacked in talent, she made up for with enthusiasm. She thought she sounded great and nothing could deter her spirit. She loved her bumble bee costume and I had difficulty getting her to take it off. As I watched her, I don't think I was prejudiced to believe she was the cutest bumble bee I ever saw as she sang and buzzed around the stage, singing.

When all the classes were finished with their singing and dancing and reading of essays, the children gathered on stage for one final bow before scurrying back to their individual classrooms. The teachers prepared the rooms for this special night, with mounted displays of the students' academic and artistic achievements.

When I arrived at Miss Needle's room, Jaime's face was glowing with excitement from her performance and the opportunity to share her classroom. She was a self-appointed greeter. Many of the visitors were Jaime groupies – parents whose children were not in

Jaime's room, but who had stopped by to meet Jaime and let her know how much they enjoyed her show. Any other child would have been put in time out or banned from all future school activities. Not Jaime. She received kudos for her outrageous solo act.

A slender, dark haired woman entered the class. Her entire demeanor was more serious than those around her. When I overheard her asking if Jaime's mother were here, I thought about climbing out a nearby window. I thought she might be the head of the PTA or on the school board. I wondered if we were about to be exiled. As she approached me she smiled and nodded toward Jaime who remained the center of attention, "She's remarkable."

This wasn't the way someone would normally begin if they were about to throw us out. I relaxed. My embarrassment left me unsure about what to say and when I found my voice I admitted, "If it had been some other child, I might be able to fully appreciate it."

"I was there when she was born and what I see today is nothing less than a miracle. I just had to come and tell you."

"You were there when Jaime was born?"

She nodded her head.

"In the delivery room?"

She nodded her head again, "I was one of the delivery-room nurses."

Now I noticed tears. Her fingers wiped at her eyes and then covered her mouth, "I only have a minute because I have to get back to my son. I shouldn't have come, but I couldn't help myself." Looking at Jaime again she said, "She's a miracle."

"You keep saying that. Is there some reason...?"

"I'm probably going to wish I never said this, but it's haunted me since she was born. Tonight was such a gift to see her. I was shocked when her teacher introduced her. She's so beautiful and doing so well, I just can't believe it." She paused and I decided to remain silent, unsure of what information was about to be forthcoming. "When she was born she had an Apgar score of 2. Do you know what that is?"

I shook my head.

"It's the way we rate how a baby is doing right after they're born. They can get a score of 10. Two points each for breathing, reflex, muscle tone, color, and heart rate. So, you know with a score of two it meant she wasn't doing well. Then he...the doctor... he...he wouldn't let us take care of her. When he saw she had Down Syndrome, he made us lay her on a table. No one was allowed to touch her. After fifteen minutes he checked and told us he guessed she was going to live, so we could clean her up. I can't tell you how many nights I haven't been able to sleep. I've always wondered what happened to her. She's beautiful. None of us believed she would make it. I wanted you to know she really is a miracle."

After delivering her message this mysterious person, who I never saw again, walked away. I never got her name. Only the message – Jaime was – is – a miracle.

Misunderstandings

Jaime spent five years in Lynn Needle's class. Through numerous Jaime adventures we had grown to appreciate one another. We became friends. On one a Friday afternoon Lynn was telling me about her home being remodeled. The construction was going to leave her without water or electricity on Saturday night. I suggested she stay at our home. Jaime was spending that night with her father and Lynn could stay in Jaime's room. She accepted my offer. Sunday morning before leaving, she wrote a note and left it on the bed thanking Jaime for allowing her to sleep there.

Monday the phone rang. It was Lynn. She sounded odd. There was a strained quality to her voice, "Uh, Linda, could you call the principal and let him know that I stayed at your house Saturday? That I slept alone in Jaime's bed?"

"Yeah. Sure. Why?" This was an odd request as we previously discussed we wouldn't tell others at the school about her staying at the house.

"Well, Jaime talked with him this morning. You know how she gets things confused? When she finished talking with him, he called me to the office and asked why I slept with Jaime's Dad in her bed this weekend."

I gasped and said, "Oh, I'm so sorry." I then groaned, but it was followed by a laugh and a giggle.

"Oh, yeah, I can tell how bad you feel for me." She began laughing, but her voice continued to be strained. It was obvious she was worried.

I called the principal and explained. He chuckled and said he believed Lynn to begin with, he was just giving her a hard time. He promised to straighten it out and I called Lynn immediately so she could relax.

Jaime often got words and concepts confused when sharing a story. Numerous times I've wondered why many people have not called to check out some outlandish statement or bizarre sounding tale. If they don't check something out, it's their problem. It took years for me to adopt this attitude. I have come to believe she helps make life interesting for people and I've learned not to worry about what they think. I am convinced that one of Jaime's goals in this lifetime is to teach others about authenticity and forgiveness. Being her mother, I am first in line for these instructions. Her lessons require humor and the tests are about love. If someone judges another person after hearing something odd about them, especially if they accept the information without checking it out, they just failed one of the love tests. Tolerance, acceptance, and a thick skin for those who don't have these attributes are major survival factors when living with a child who has special needs.

Wrong Move

The time came for Jaime to leave Miss Needle's class and I was faced with another decision. She made considerable progress with her socialization skills. School officials were encouraging me to transfer her to regular education classes at the local junior high school. They promised if she didn't like it, she could return. I talked with Jaime about what it would mean to go to a new school and a different type of program. We visited the school. She decided she wanted to try something new. Nothing ventured, nothing gained.

Mr. Schaffer, the school Vice Principal, began calling the first week of her attendance at the middle school. He wanted to keep me posted on Jaime's progress and reported her newest antics. Unlike Miss Needle, he was not amused. By the second month, I received an invitation to come to his office. It did not make me feel special. His office and its furniture looked like their occupant, stark and angular. His greeting was formal and his handshake as thin and flat as his smile. Small talk was not his forte. He started immediately with the problem, "Jaime's had difficulty adjusting. I'm not sure this is the right place for her."

"Really? Why?" His almost daily phone calls would have been sufficient to alert anyone, but not pleased with the way he was handling this, I didn't want to give him an easy out.

"Well, for example, she isolates herself." It always hurts to hear that your child is left out of activities. However, his next comment pulled me out of sadness. The conflicting messages sent warning signals up my spine. "And she's overly friendly. She wrote this note to one of the boys." He handed me a piece of paper with block lettering on it that read:

I LIKE YOU

LOVE

JAIME JOHNSON

After looking at the paper, I could remember writing similar notes to boys when I was a young girl. I was glad no one called my mother. I laid it back on his desk and ask, "Do you call all the parents in when you find a note like this?"

"Uh, no, but this was different."

"Because?"

"Jaime's different."

Deciding to play dumb, I responded, "I don't understand. Was I called because you're concerned she isolates herself or because she's too friendly? How can she be both?"

"Well, she sits by herself at lunch, but other times she approaches students when they don't want her to. I mean, she will even come right up to me and give me a hug."

"Is that right? Well, Mr. Schaffer, that is one of the wonderful things about children like Jaime, they are capable of loving the unlovable." I then smiled brightly.

Mr. Schaffer nodded his head in agreement and just as quickly a strange look crossed his face as he fully processed what had just been said. Would a parent ever be so bold as to make such a statement on purpose? Certainly not this pleasant young woman sitting in front of him smiling. But I had. It was the truth. And the truth made me happy. Jaime has always been capable of loving the unlovable.

Jaime's capacity to love far exceeded the average person's. She seemed to receive her love from a nuclear source. It was her genius and yet it could not be measured in the academic arena. I would not have it drained or shut down by people who had no understanding or appreciation of her. One thing the Vice Principal and I agreed on – this was not the right place for Jaime. Immediate calls were made to request a transfer back to special education.

It took six months for the transfer to take place. During that time Jaime regressed sufficiently to lose one to two years of hard earned skills in every subject. And yet, when she was back in a class offering safety and security, and with her self-esteem restored, she bloomed. Within six months she had quickly regained the lost skills.

It's a federal law that children with special needs are to be offered the least restrictive environment. For Jaime that was a special education classroom with intermittent opportunities for mainstreaming. Regular education had been too demanding and harsh for her to thrive. It was truly a school of hard knocks – a demeaning experience.

Many times over the years parents have asked me what to do about their child's education. Every child is unique and each year of their life presents new challenges. Much depends on the teacher. I wish I could clone Miss Needle and some of the other wonderful teachers in Jaime's life. On the other hand, some of the teachers never should have gone into special education, like Miss Saunders, her first teacher, and two of my other least favorites – Mr. Binder and Miss Dorsey.

Mr. Binder was one of the additional reasons for removing Jaime from Mayfield Junior High School. Like most children with Down Syndrome, speech problems have always been an issue for Jaime. Her issues included a minor stuttering problem. In special education the therapist worked with her three times a week and sent home information sheets so I could practice with her. When she moved to junior high no speech therapist was in sight. During one of Mr. Schaffer's calls I mentioned speech therapy and he said her teacher, Mr. Binder, was holding group speech lessons until they could get a speech therapist. Jaime's stuttering increased tremendously. I went to the classroom to discuss it and met with her teacher, "Mr. B-B-B-B-Bi-iin-d-d-der." I knew immediately why Jaime's stuttering was worse. She loves imitating people. He had the worst stuttering problem I ever encountered.

This might not be a major issue for most teachers. But for a special education teacher in this district, at this time, with me as Jaime's mother, it was huge. I called the school district office and asked where I should send the bill for a private speech therapist. The polite secretary said I couldn't do that. I told the woman to read the Individual Education Program rights. She checked with the Director, who called me back within five minutes and requested a meeting. They found a speech therapist to start working with Jaime immediately. It's unusual for Jaime to stutter anymore, unless she becomes nervous. When that happens, I think of Mr. Binder. I hope and pray that he found a different position before he ruined any other children's speech.

Then there was Miss Dorsey. Thank goodness she was only a summer substitute. I received a call about the time Jaime's bus usually arrived home. It was Miss Dorsey, "Uh, Mrs. Johnson uh, we'll be bringing Jaime home in a car today."

"Oh? Did something happen?"

"Well, uh, nothing serious. I mean, uh, she's okay and everything."

"And?"

"Well, you know we went to the fair today, right?"

"Yes?"

"Well, you, uh, know how independent Jaime is, right?"

It began to feel very uncomfortable, like I was extracting teeth instead of information; and I was not sure I should be agreeing with everything. "Yeah?"

"Just as we were all ready to leave, she left the group and went to the bathroom, without telling anyone." There was a long pause, "She was still there when we got on the bus... uh... she's okay... we didn't know it until we got back to the school... she really is okay... the police have her at the fair. They bought her ice cream."

She laughed. I didn't. She left my child at the fair. Jaime was okay, but she had been left at the fair. What does a mother do with information like this? I called the Director and made sure he was aware that a child, my child, had been abandoned at the fair. It was my heartfelt desire that I never saw Miss Dorsey again after summer school. And I didn't.

What did Jaime do about being left at the fair? She came home with a big smile and when asked, "How was your day?"

She responded, "Fun day!"

"Miss Dorsey called me. She told me they left you at the fair. Were you afraid when you came out of the bathroom and you couldn't find your class?"

Her eyes filled with tears, she nodded, and then she smiled, "I cry. Police. Help me. Ice cream. I okay. I be happy." She then gave me a big hug. She was feeling safe. She was home. She hugged harder. I felt tears on my cheeks, I wasn't sure if they were hers or mine.

Moments like these make all the bad ones seem insignificant. They speak to the essence of the education which Jaime brought into my life. We live, explore, struggle, learn, think, feel, communicate, cry, laugh, and most importantly, love. Everything is secondary to the relationships we have in our lives... and the love... and the decision to be happy.

— IV —

Friends

Some people come into our lives and quickly go. Some stay for a while and leave footprints on our hearts.

~Anonymous

Big Trouble

Many neighborhood children were friendly with Jaime, but her first real friendships developed when she joined Miss Needle's class. Jaime's best friend was Katie, a tiny blonde, every inch of her filled with dynamic energy. The two loved running circles around people, literally. Their second favorite activity was telling on each other.

One day stands out in my mind. Jaime ran in the door, dropped her school bag, and yelled, "Mom, Mom!"

"I'm right here...in the kitchen."

As she entered the kitchen she said, "Mom. Katie. Katie in trouble. Big trouble."

"What happened?"

"She not allowed on bus. No more. Ever." Now her eyes filled with tears at the idea that her best friend would no longer be riding the bus with her. Banned forever from school transportation. Knowing Jaime, I could tell she was trying to process beyond that – how would Katie be getting to school? Would she be allowed to come to school? Would she ever see her friend again?

I held out my arms. She ran to me and threw her arms around me. I could feel her silent sobs. After several minutes, when she was quiet, she let go, backed away, and looked at me with fear in her hazel eyes. Her lips trembled slightly, "Katie in big trouble."

"What did Katie do?"

Somberly Jaime looked at me, stepped back, and held up her right hand, palm facing me. She then looked at the floor, made a face and daringly looked back at me and said, "She did this!" At that point she pushed her hand further toward me and made a fist, with the exception of extending a finger, her index finger. She did it again with emphasis and serious expression of someone angry and giving another person "the finger." With her index finger still extended, pointing at the ceiling, she extended her arm once again toward me, "She did 'this' to bus driver!"

I couldn't help myself, I burst out laughing. Jaime knew that wasn't the response she should have received. Puzzled, she looked at her hand, and said, "Oh! I mean, 'this!'" With that she turned her hand around so it was no longer palm facing me, but now the back of her hand with the index finger extended upward. Now she was smiling, sure she got it right.

I quickly decided not to let her know that she 'had it wrong' and frowned at her, "That's not nice, Jaime. You know Katie was just kicked off the bus for that. I don't ever want to see you do that again."

Jaime quickly dropped her hand, holding it behind her back, as if the hand itself was naughty. She hated disappointing anyone. I never saw her do "that" again, but often smile when I think of her, gesturing with an angry look, while pointing at the sky.

Jaime never asked what that gesture meant. It made me realize there are many things about raising a child with a disability that are easier than raising children without disabilities. Katie returned to riding the bus within a month. The bus driver reported overhearing Jaime talking with Katie, "No more finger, Katie. You stay on bus. I miss you...okay? Promise... no more finger. Okay, Katie? Promise... I like you... I miss you... okay?" It must have worked. Katie stayed on the bus.

First Courting

Before Jay left to live with his father, Jaime and Jay often had friends visit our home. The most memorable of Jaime's visitors drove up on a Friday afternoon about four o'clock in a yellow Volkswagen beetle. He was absolutely adorable, all four and a half feet of him. A small-framed, blue-eyed blonde boy, with hair slicked back on each side and across the top. He climbed out of the driver's side of the car, strutted up the sidewalk, and rang the bell. When I opened the door, he proudly asked for Jaime.

Curious about this child who was driving a car, I responded, "Who may I tell her is calling?"

"Corey. She should be expecting me. I asked her out and she said 'yes.'"

Jaime had said nothing about any Corey or a date or anything. Feeling a burst of parental protection, I blurted out, "Well, she didn't ask me and won't be able to go. She isn't even here right now." After unleashing my initial emotional reaction, I began to gain a sense of perspective, and decided to get some information about this young, errant Casanova, "Corey, that's a nice car, where did you get it?"

He proudly puffed up as he half-turned to glance at the car and reported, "It's my brother's. He loaned it to me for my date."

"How old are you?" I knew he could not be more than eleven or twelve.

He didn't like the way the questions were going and he probably didn't like the tone of my voice. His ice blue eyes narrowed and his face turned incredibly mean and cold. That one look told volumes. Driving was not the only thing he experienced that went beyond his age. I wanted to find out more than a first name, "Uh, if you give me your phone number, I'll have Jaime call you. I'm sure she'll be disappointed that she missed you."

He stood there a moment considering what to do, but I had already made him suspicious with my last question, "Nah, I'll call her. She shoulda' been here, you know? We had a date. She promised."

"How did you meet Jaime?" I wasn't going to give up. I had to find out where he came from, who he was.

"School. We met at school. She's a nice girl, but she shoulda' been here." With that he turned and was gone. He climbed into his little yellow VW and drove away.

I immediately called the police and reported a young child driving a yellow VW. They never called back. Corey never called again. When I talked with Jaime she said she didn't remember any Corey. The date must not have been high on her priority list or I am sure she would have been waiting in the front yard and gone before I knew what happened to her. It is such a frightening thought, especially remembering the icy look that Corey delivered in response to a question he didn't like.

First thing the next morning, I notified the school. The principal knew who Corey was and promised to keep a closer watch on Jaime when she was interacting with students other than her own class at recess and lunch.

I worked with Jaime to help her understand "stranger-danger," but, it is a difficult concept for a child who loves everyone. She struggles with the idea that not all people she meets in safe places are safe, and not all friendly people are friends. Corey was one example, but not the first and certainly not the last.

Like every mother, I wish I could keep Jaime in a protective bubble, but she has her own lessons to learn. Like most children, she will stubbornly ignore parental advice and be taught by trial and error.

No matter how much a mother may want to make her child's decisions to save her from the pain of ignorance and naïveté, it will never work. I understand that being overly protective has a lasting and somewhat crippling effect on a child. No matter how much I might worry, I recognized this as the truth for Jaime and often struggle to allow her as much autonomy as possible. I tell myself that raising a child with special needs is no more difficult than raising any other child. Every child needs to learn to make decisions and become stronger through their mistakes. It is a painful process, but it is worth it. Jaime has a strong sense of self, of right and wrong, and no one can change her mind once it's made up.

Party Time

Our home often appeared to be Grand Central Station. It seemed there was always someone visiting. The children in the neighborhood seemed to gravitate to our home, as did my friends, who came from a myriad of backgrounds. Some people attract stray animals; we had a way of attracting people who seemed to be lost in the fray of life.

Jaime's exposure to many diverse individuals produced the least prejudiced person I know. She is blind to age, color, disability, sexuality, or economic level. She just loves people. In turn, others seem to sense her unconditional love and feel good about being around her. My friends always accept her, or they don't remain friends. She's like an amulet that keeps negative people out of my life.

Jaime loves to have fun. Mention "party" and she is dressed and ready. Any excuse will do, and it doesn't matter who is invited. She always finds a way to blend in and enjoy herself. Given a theme, she decorates every inch of the house. If someone is needed to fix or serve food, she volunteers. One of Jaime's favorite party jobs is greeting people. She also loves monitoring the music and makes sure it is never ending. She is, indeed, a party animal.

At the same time, she never stops observing what is happening. She seems to understand that if she is busy doing something, people aren't as likely to notice they are being watched. She constantly gathers information for enriching her imitations. They never know when they will have the opportunity to see themselves from Jaime's perspective. When she sees someone or something she finds amusing, she will disappear for a while and return wearing something similar, and will imitate aspects of their personality or reenact something they did. Friends are often amazed and amused with Jaime's theatrical exhibits.

At times, new friends find some of Jaime's actions disconcerting. Her blatant honesty is unprecedented. It is the underlying inspiration for many of her actions. For example, when she thinks it is time for someone to go home, she will bring their coat to them. New visitors are often unsure of how to act with Jaime's cloak delivery service as she plops their wraps in their laps. Old friends learn to laugh, lay their coats to the side, and give her a hug. Jaime is not someone who likes her plans to be derailed, but when everyone remains neutral about the coat delivery, her response is often one of total disgust at "grown-ups" who just don't understand anything.

She desperately does not want to miss out on anything, so she doesn't want to retire until everyone leaves. In response to being ignored Jaime will turn on her heel and swiftly make a dramatic exit. This doesn't mean she's gone. Many times she has been known to return shortly after being dismissed, dressed in janitorial garb, ready for party clean up. Her appearance and performance would rival Carol Burnett's cleaning woman.

If anyone stubbornly remains after her cleaning act, she will again disappear for a short time. Upon her return she frequently offers a private fashion show, swirling and twirling in her fanciest pajamas. Then with one great final bow and curtsy, she exits for the night. Only the sound of giggles can be heard trailing behind her, and just before she closes her door she says, "I be happy!"

— V —

We are Family

Call it a clan, call it a tribe, call it a family:
Whatever you call it, whoever you are, you need one.
~ Jane Howard

A Little Child Shall Lead

From the time Jaime entered my life I was never sure who was learning from whom. It felt as if we were piloting a mutual mentoring program. I knew I was the parent and she was the child, but there was always so much happening in, around, and through our lives with new challenges and lessons, it seemed both of us were perpetual students. I remain in awe at Jaime's never ending drive, tenacity and joyful attitude; it makes me look up to her while looking down at her. She often gives me the will to keep going even when I want to give up.

The beginning of 1984 was brutal. The first week in January I lost my job. Kathey, the woman who lived with me, also lost her job. We had no money coming in to pay bills or buy food. It was the coldest winter on record. The temperatures had dropped drastically to below zero, and with the wind chill factor it was colder than anyone could imagine. In the midst of the artic weather, our furnace broke down. We had no money to get it fixed. It was a bitter time. We brought electric blankets to the kitchen, turned the oven on and sat around the stove. Jaime led a song fest. We fixed popcorn. She called it a "party," a "fun time."

Jaime absolutely insisted we go to church, even when I least felt like it. During that long cold winter she frequently reminded me, "Pray God, Mom. Pray God. Be okay."

I applied for numerous jobs. Winter dragged on. I became less and less hopeful, but Jaime's faith never wavered. She was the one who kept me strong until I finally found a job and things started turning around. Jaime continued to be consistent in her faith and her desire to attend church, "Thank God, Mom. Thank God." The church became an integral part of our lives.

During a statewide ARC meeting which was very well attended, I attempted to share some of my ideas. However, when I spoke up to make my point about promoting better care for the special needs population, my voice wavered and cracked. It was frustrating and embarrassing, and I felt my ideas were lost due to an inability to express myself effectively. The entire presentation seemed inept and weak. So I started attending our church's Toastmaster's group as a way to learn about public speaking. My social life was limited to a smattering of ARC meetings once or twice a month, Toastmasters, and church.

During that winter it took every ounce of strength I had to keep going. I felt like the walking dead, at least emotionally. When spring arrived we celebrated being released from the depths of the winter of despair. The warmth of spring and a new job brought rays of hope. I started to believe we would be okay. In preparation for Easter, Jaime and I went shopping. She called it, "Ladies' day – a fun day." We splurged and prepared to make ourselves beautiful; it was our renewal celebration.

The sky was such a rich blue color. If it had been a painting, you would say it was too perfect to be realistic. It was the kind of day that makes a person want to lie down on the grass and watch the clouds float by. As much as I might have wanted to do that, we were on our way to church. I loved the church from the first time I walked into it. It was plainly constructed in the shape of a pyramid, primarily wood, with windows at the top which allowed rays of reflected sunlight to stream down and dance around inside the church. Like most people who attend church regularly, I had a favorite area where I would normally sit, about half way to the front on the left side. When we arrived, I looked toward our usual seats and pointed to them, Jaime led the way.

At the row where we usually turned in, she looked at me for approval. I nodded my head. The man on the end stood up to let us pass. We walked in about three seats when Jaime suddenly stopped. I almost ran over her. She leaned over the seat in front of her and kissed the man who was sitting there. I was astonished that she would do such a thing. She had never kissed a stranger before. Then, as if it was the most natural thing in the world, she turned and kept walking. The man turned and smiled. I didn't know what to say, so I didn't say anything.

I had seen this man at Toastmasters. There was something about him. Of all the men in the world, why did Jaime kiss him? We finally got to our seats. I leaned over to Jaime, "Why did you kiss that man?"

She shrugged. She was digging in her purse and seemed oblivious. My friend, Kathey, was chuckling and whispered, "That was worth coming to church for."

The man half turned, looked back, and smiled again. I looked down, embarrassed. I wanted to disappear. I thought about grabbing Jaime's arm and quickly whisking her out through the other aisle, but figured that would draw more attention. I was in church, so I decided the best thing to do would be to pray about this. "Dear God, why did she stop and kiss that man? You know I saw him for the first time at Toastmaster's the day after I lost my job in January. You know that I have been attracted to him, but the last thing I need in my life right now is a man. And out of all the men in this church, why in the world would she stop and kiss *that* one?" By then I was holding my head in my hands.

Kathey and I had been through a lot. She knew when things were not right. She leaned over and asked, "Are you okay?"

I nodded, but couldn't bring myself to lift my head. Tears had formed. I didn't want anyone to see.

By then, Jaime joined in, "Mom? You okay?"

Another nod and a deep breath. I pushed my hands against my eyes and raised my head, with a final swipe across my cheek, I smiled and nodded.

Looking at Jaime, "I don't want you kissing strange men."

"Okay." She looked hurt.

Kathey leaned in and whispered, "There's more to this than a stranger. Is he the guy from Toastmasters?"

I shook my head in denial. I was mad at myself for having mentioned seeing this man at Toastmaster's. I certainly didn't want her to know this really was that man. It was too bizarre already. I loved this church, the ministers and their sermons. That morning I never heard a word of the service. I couldn't wait until it was over. Immediately afterward, Kathey said, "Let's find that man and apologize to him during social time."

I curtly responded, "We have to go. We have things to do today. Let's hurry up." I saw the man walking toward us. I turned and quickly exited in the opposite direction.

In the following weeks, we sat in a different area of the church. I watched carefully to avoid getting close to the man Jaime kissed.

The first week in May I gave the opening greeting at the Toastmasters' meeting. I almost completed it when my heart began pounding like I had just run an Olympic race. Public speaking had become comfortable for me over the past year, so that was not the problem. It was the man who entered late during my presentation. He was tall, well over six feet, had broad shoulders, and carried himself in a manner that offered no apology for being late. Distinguished gray hair and a mustache complemented his teasing, hazel eyes that never once lost their intent gaze. His presence seemed to fill the room and no matter where I looked, I continued to see him if only from the corner of my eye. A slight smile touched his lips each time our eyes connected.

Not since grade school had I been so relieved to complete a presentation and return to my chair. There was no doubt in my mind, if I turned and looked, the man would be looking at me. I could feel him looking at me. This was the man Jaime kissed on Easter Sunday. I thought about leaving early, but I had come with a neighbor, Nina. Immediately following the meeting I connected with several friends and went into one of the private offices. After finishing our business, we returned to the main room. Most of the people were gone and I gave a sigh of relief until I heard a man standing behind me say, "Oh, there you are."

Before I turned I knew who it was and I knew he was talking to me. My heart leapt. I closed my eyes for a second to gain a sense of balance and perspective. How could this be happening? Turning my head toward the voice, "Are you talking to me?"

His eyes were now dancing, "I believe I am. Can I get you a cup of coffee?"

"I'm going to look for my friend who should be in the kitchen, if you want to come with me." Geesh! That sounded stupid. I hadn't even answered him. Why didn't I just say I'll get my own darned coffee?

He followed me to the kitchen in my search for Nina, who immediately brightened when she noted the hulk of a man behind me. Nina was not known for her shyness, "Well, hello, aren't you the handsome one? What's your name?"

He laughed, "Finally, someone who wants to meet me. I'm Ed. Ed Tuttle. And you?"

"Nina." She held out her hand, which he accepted and gently shook before nodding at me, "And your friend, does she have a name?"

"I thought you two knew each other when you came in together." Looking at me, "Should I tell him?"

"If he wants to know he should ask."

Ed laughed, "I don't think I ever worked so hard for a name. Promise me you'll go out with me for my efforts."

I shook my head.

"Okay, at least tell me your name."

"Linda."

"Beautiful. Linda means beautiful. Now, go out with me...please."

I groaned.

Nina was enjoying the show. She began applauding, "Yes! Yes! For such a performance he deserves you." I turned and gave her a look that should have calmed her. Instead she escalated, "Go for it, Linda."

I did a quick assessment of the situation. He was persistent. That was an important attribute. He had a sense of humor. That was even more important. His smile brought life back into perspective. Life had been out of kilter for a long while. He was a handsome man. It might be time to improve the scenery of my life. He attended church regularly. Jaime kissed him.

"Just one glass of wine?" His question broke into my thoughts.

My response surprised me, "Okay, one, but only one."

Even though I accepted the invitation, I was not convinced it was a wise thing to do. Ed was older and everything about him was self-assured, maybe too self assured. As we walked across the parking lot, we approached a dark green Jaguar sedan. As he opened the door, he was obviously proud of it and all I wanted to do was turn around and run, find Nina and go home. A Jaguar! He was one of those men. I never liked the type of man who found prestige in a car, and rarely did they like me – I was too independent, too outspoken, and had two children.

As I got into the car I noticed a sign on the glove compartment, "Thank You for Not Smoking." Great! Strike two and we aren't out of the parking lot. Smoking was my one vice and I had no intention of giving it up for a man. He got into the car and said, "I can't believe it's May and it's still cold. I just moved from California."

A crazy Californian! Third strike! I looked at the door handle and wondered how I could bail before it was too late. I was almost sure Nina had already left. If I jumped out of the car, I could end up being stranded in the almost empty church parking lot at night. Darn. I decided to go through with my agreement – one drink.

The conversation flowed easily and effortlessly, which was amazing considering that my fears were motivating me to seek out his faults and flaws. He chose one of my favorite restaurants, The Wine Cellar. We found seating that offered privacy near the piano bar where a friend of mine entertained with soft jazz tunes. The pianist noticed us as we walked in. He nodded and smiled. Ed and I had just settled in when my friend announced, "This one is for my friend who just came in." He then played "Linda," a well known tune from the 1940's. Ed immediately joined in and quietly sang, "When I go to sleep, I never count sheep, I count all the charms about Linda." He had a deep voice and carried the tune well. My face was unaccustomed to shades of red, but I could feel the color rising up my neck and into my cheeks.

Ed's next comment was typical of what someone would expect from a Californian. I heard there were men who used it as a pickup line, "What sign are you?"

I thought about it and decided to continue to give him a bad time. I had studied astrology for close to ten years. Sitting back in my seat, I smiled sweetly, thinking I would teach him a lesson about asking a girl her sign. "Well, you know you can't just go by a sun sign. My sun is in Libra, moon in Scorpio, ascendant is Aquarius. My Mercury is in Libra and my Venus, Mars and Jupiter are all in Scorpio. Would you like to know more?"

"Wow! That's terrific. I am a Sagittarius with my moon in Leo and a Libra ascendant. That must have been the immediate attraction." He then went on to sketch out his entire chart.

I was speechless.

He smiled, "It's obvious you've studied some astrology. I'll bet you thought it was just a line to ask about your sign."

The color red returned to my face and he was noticeably amused. He shared that he had also studied astrology for ten years. It doesn't take much to have two astrologers engage in a deep conversation. Our time together went by quickly. The glass of wine was empty and I found myself surprised at not wanting the evening to end. My internal force field, which I developed to keep the male species at bay, began crumbling. I liked this man who Jaime selected for her kiss.

We soon learned we had many common interests. It appeared we were compatible. And yet I didn't want to give up my preconceived ideas about him being an ostentatious Californian. Learning how much we shared, created a common ground. I found myself looking forward to knowing more about this man. That one night led to spending nearly every evening together, thereafter. I couldn't seem to help myself. I was immediately in love... deeply... completely. No questions asked. It was as if we had always been together. As if we had spent our lives preparing ourselves for one another.

Ed was not thwarted by my independent and forthright nature. He actually enjoyed my passion and sincerity and encouraged unvarnished conversations when we had differing views. This alone unsettled and won favor from my rebellious spirit, which was not used to being so easily accepted.

Ed had no previous experience with children who had developmental delays or mental retardation. He wasn't sure what to expect. When he brought me home from our first date he had the opportunity to experience Jaime's impish nature. We were sitting in front of the house having a lively discussion about the benefits of California versus Ohio when the front porch light began flickering off and on, off and on, off and on. He said, "Who's that? Does your mother live with you?"

"That would be my daughter."

"Aren't the roles reversed?"

"More often than you might imagine. She won't stop, so I'm going in. Do you want to come with me?"

"Not tonight. Is this the young lady who kissed me in church?"

Oh, my God, he remembered! He hadn't said anything all night and I assumed he hadn't remembered, but he did. For a moment I thought about acting like I didn't know what he was talking about and then thought how silly that would be. "Uh, yeah. That's Jaime."

"Great. I'm looking forward to meeting her when I pick you up on Wednesday, right?"

Our first date was May 10, 1984. On June 13, 1984, Ed proposed. I accepted. We were both surprised. We had been single for a long time and neither of us had planned to ever marry again. However, in September I became Mrs. Edward Tuttle.

From the time Ed and I met, our lives were in a constant state of adjustment, as if we had entered a different dimension. I learned that Ed was a business owner and a minister. Within a month of his marriage proposal, he accepted a local church pulpit. So, while we were making preparations for joining our lives, I was trying to adapt to the concept of being married to a minister and adjusting to the role of being a minister's wife. Jaime loved the church and our involvement with the activities. I often thought she might have been better suited to the role of a minister's wife.

Ed made his own adjustments to settling down to family life in the Midwest, complete with two women, me and Kathey, and a special-needs child who chose him out of three hundred people in a church service.

The first time Ed came to the house Jaime did not seem to remember that he was "the one" she had kissed at the church. She was polite, but didn't seem to pay much attention to him. Then two events happened that removed any doubts about our being a family.

It was Father's Day and Jaime had been invited to have dinner at her dad's home. She prepared by purchasing Carl a gift and buying him a card. Two hours before he was to pick Jaime up, he called to say that something had come up and he wouldn't be able to get her. Broken hearted, Jaime began to cry. She brought his gift to me and said, "Daddy gift. Give him. Please."

Carl had moved almost an hour away, but I couldn't say no to her plea. I called Carl and shared that Jaime had a gift and card for him, would it be okay if she stopped for a minute to give it to him?

His response will remain with me forever, "No, we have company. Mom and Dad are here."

Carl's parents lived four blocks from us. They drove by our home to go to Carl's. They made a decision not to include Jaime in their family's Father's Day celebration. I held the phone for awhile after he hung up. I couldn't bear to look anywhere other than the blank wall that held the phone. A primal scream was stuck, somewhere between my heart and throat. What had just happened made no sense. There was absolutely no justification for the cruelty of Carl's actions, or inaction. I had to tell Jaime. What could I tell her? That her father, whom she deeply loved, didn't want to share Father's Day with her? Wouldn't allow us to even bring a gift and card to him?

Jaime tugged at my sleeve, "Mom? We go see Daddy?"

Ed walked in and knew immediately that something was wrong, "Linda, are you okay?"

I nodded and reached out to pull Jaime close to me. As I hugged her, silent tears slid down my cheeks. Ed enfolded both of us with his arms, "What a great Father's Day for me, to be with two special ladies." He gently touched my face and brushed the tears away. "Let's do something special."

Jaime looked at me and said, "Daddy?"

I cleared my throat, "Uh, Daddy said he isn't going to be home."

She began sobbing. I held her. Ed intervened once again, "Why don't we go out and do something fun?"

Jaime nodded as her tears subsided, "I go dress." She disappeared into her bedroom. When she returned she held out a piece of paper to Ed. Her printing was large and plain, "Happy Father's Day, Daddy Ed. I Love You, Jaime."

Holding the paper, Ed's face turned red. His eyes brimmed with tears. Another hug was in order. As he took Jaime into his arms he told her, "I love you, too. You're a wonderful daughter."

Jaime disappeared once again and when she returned she was carrying the present she purchased for Carl. She laid it in front of Ed, "For you." Both Ed and I tried to dissuade her, but she was insistent. "You my new dad." There was a shift for all of us that day. We had become a family, the type of family that faces unpleasant situations and makes the best of them. Ed was the "new dad."

Jaime had what is referred to as a lazy eye. She needed surgery. Ed went with us to the hospital and supported me during the long wait while Jaime was in surgery. He was always careful not to be too intrusive, so when she came out of recovery he suggested I see her alone. I walked into the room and she immediately asked for Ed.

When he walked in, Jaime, from an anesthetic haze, reached out her hand and called to him in a slow groggy voice, "Ed, Ed. Ed, Ed." He took her hand. There was no question in any of our minds that we all belonged together. We may have seemed like the "odd family," but being together worked for us. And the rest of the world would have to adjust. What fate had in store for us was yet to be seen.

Prodigal Sons

In the midst of adjusting to one another, marriage, purchasing a home, business demands, and church expectations, Ed's teenage son Bryan who lived with his mother in California decided to move to Ohio and join our family. Within weeks of Bryan's arrival, I received a call from my son, Jay. There had been a major altercation with his father and Martha. He wanted to live with us. When I learned the details, it wasn't even necessary to consult with Ed, "Sure, Jay, this is your home. Should we pick you up?"

"No. Dad said he will bring me over."

When I replaced the phone in its cradle I was aware of a mixture of sad-glad feelings. My child was separating from his father. His dreams and their promises had never materialized, but I knew his decision to return had not been an easy one. Martha and Carl had become abusive; and no mother wants her child to be hurt. My heart was heavy with the pain of events that brought him back, but, he was coming home. I felt nothing but unadulterated joy at that prospect.

A memory crossed my mind. It was 1982 and Jay had been living with Carl and Martha for a while. He was home one weekend just after the movie "ET" had been released and Jaime said it would be a "fun day" to go to the show. Jay invited his friend, Jason, and spirits were high. Laughter filled the car as we pulled into the parking lot.

As we drove closer to the theater we saw a long line of people. The laughter stopped. My heart dropped. I shared my thoughts, "Shoot, it never occurred to me we might not be able to get tickets." A wave of sadness enveloped me as I placed my head on the steering wheel. It only lasted a moment when, I straightened up and said, "Does anyone still want to try to do this today?"

The children let out a resounding, "Yes!"

I smiled at their youthful optimism and exuberance, "Okay, Jay and Jason, hop out and see if you can get tickets."

Jaime and I found a convenient parking space where we could watch the boys slowly move toward the ticket window. It was finally their turn. They stayed there a long time. Jay turned around and looked toward the car. His expression told it all. We would not be going to the movies today.

I felt bad and commented to Jaime, "Darn, I wish I had planned ahead."

Just then Jay smiled and broke into a dance as he held up four tickets and waved at us to join them. I groaned as I said, "That brother of yours loves to tease us." Jaime laughed with delight.

The show was as good as we'd hoped it would be. "ET" was an endearing, lovable character who engendered audience interactions as his adventure unfolded. People laughed and cheered during moments of victory and cried when ET's sadness grew with his yearning to return home. Back in the car Jay and Jason were typical twelve year-olds, imitating different characters. Jaime, who was in the front seat, turned around and stuck her finger over the seat toward the boys. In her best ET voice she squeaked, "ET come home." She peeked around the seat, stretched her short little arm and finger as far as it would extend and again using her crackly ET voice said, "Jay come home...Jay come home."

Jay and Jason roared with laughter. Jay looked at Jaime and held his finger out, continuing to laugh loudly. He was laughing so hard he was gasping for air. He covered his face. I looked in the mirror and saw huge tears running down his cheeks. His laughter turned to sobs. Jaime, once again reaching back as far as she could, said, "Jay come home." Now she started weeping. She used her own voice to say again, "Please, Jay, come home."

I wiped away the tears that always accompanied that memory. Jay was finally coming home. Jaime would be ecstatic. I wished it had been under different circumstances.

With Jay's arrival we had a full house and a little fine-tuning to do. We now had three teenagers who were very different in temperament and personality living together – with us – in the same home. It was good that Ed was a minister. Prayer became an increasingly important part of my life.

The boys intermittently attended church services and special events. The church attracted a number of artsy people and a variety of gifted musicians, so they decided to coordinate a talent show. They even made space for comedy and improvisations. Everyone attended.

Each performer seemed better than the last. The show was a huge success, better than we'd ever hoped it might be, and when the entertainers came together for their final bows, the audience kept applauding and asking for more. The musicians gave in to the popular demand and decided to continue after a short break.

Searching the church center, we found the boys in the kitchen area, stuffing their faces with homemade chocolate chip cookies. I said, "Hey, guys, we're tired and Ed still needs to prepare his sermon for tomorrow.

Are you going to stay and listen to more music or are you coming home?"

After checking in with each other Bryan shared, "We're going to stay. And don't say it, I promise to drive carefully."

We found Jaime in the main room. She indicated she also wanted to stay, so we said our goodbyes to everyone and left.

When we arrived home it didn't take long to change into pajamas. Ed began working on his sermon and I read a book. The phone rang at eleven thirty. It startled both of us. I hadn't realized it was so late and commented to Ed, "Why don't you get that? It has to be the boys. They probably want to go somewhere else. Please tell them to come home."

Ed picked up the phone, "Hello." A strange look came over his face, with some pauses between comments, the only words he said were, "Oh, really? Uh-huh."

My heart began to race.

Then he said, "We'll be there in fifteen minutes." He hung up the phone and looked at me. He seemed puzzled, "Did you make arrangements for the boys to bring Jaime home?"

"Well, yes. I asked if they were planning to stay and they said yes. I didn't specifically ask them about Jaime. Why? What's happened?"

Ed smiled, "You're in big trouble. I mean with a capital 'T.' That was Cindy and Bob. They stayed to clean up the church and want to know what to do with Jaime."

"What? Where are the boys?"

Ed shrugged his shoulders, "I guess they left a while ago. Everyone thought we would be back to pick Jaime up. I guess we better do it."

The minute we pulled in front of the church, the door flew open and Jaime ran out. She grabbed the car door, threw it open, and yelled, "Why you leave me?!" She rapidly climbed into the car as if we might leave her again if she was too slow.

Bob and Cindy followed her out of the building. They were smiling as Cindy said, "Someone is not happy, but she had a great time until she realized you weren't here to take her home."

Embarrassed, I half smiled and responded, "I'm sorry. I don't know what happened. We thought the boys would bring her home. Have you seen the boys?"

The look that Bob and Cindy shared told the story. No one knew when the boys left, but they were waiting for us when we got home. Jay met us at the door, "Where were you?"

"Oh, I think that is a question you have to answer. We had to go back to the church to pick up your sister, who you two should have brought home."

Jay looked at Bryan, who looked confused, "Nobody said anything about Jaime."

I stopped just inside the door and looked at the whole family. "I'm too tired to sort this out tonight. It never dawned on me that you two would leave and not bring Jaime with you."

"We didn't even know she was there!"

"How could that possibly be, the place isn't all that big."

Jay spoke first, "Right after you left, we decided to go out and get something to eat. We never went back to the main room. We never knew Jaime was there. You didn't tell us you were leaving her."

Jaime chimed in with a forlorn look on her face, "Mom, you leave me." Her chin quivered, tears filled her eyes, "Why leave me? You no love me?"

I gathered her in my arms as the boys decided to be brotherly with comments like, "That's right, Jaime, nobody loves you. That's why we left you."

"You two stop it right now. Everyone loves you, Jaime. It was a mistake. Don't be sad."

She sniffed and looked at me, "You no leave me...ever." She buried her head in my chest, looked sideways at the boys and stuck her tongue out at them, "Mom love me best."

The boys yelled objections and everyone started laughing. We were okay. No one was left out of the fun. I have learned over the years never to try to reassure Jaime by saying, "I've never left you." Also, no one should ever ask Jaime if she was left behind. If she lives to be a hundred, bearing a sad, forlorn look and in her best Sarah Bernhardt manner, she will tell whoever she can that her mother left her at the church.

Big Changes

Our full house lasted for two years. The first change occurred when Bryan made a decision to return to California. It was a pattern for him to move back and forth, spending six months or a year with each parent. We were pleased he stayed for two years.

Shortly after Bryan left, Jay announced that his father and Martha had asked for another chance. Intellectually, I understood his need to repair his relationship with them, but my inner world fell victim to a violent emotional storm. Totally devastated, I surrendered, knowing that Jay required this for his personal growth, his maturity. Going through heart surgery would have been easier than releasing him to return to people who had been so mean. There were no indications they had changed. But once again, they won his trust by playing to his sensitive nature, begging for forgiveness, and making more promises, although they would prove to be empty promises that held little hope of ever becoming a reality.

The decision plagued Jay; his pain was obvious. He isolated himself, played loud music, walked around the house without interacting or talking, and was frequently teary eyed. I did not want to add to his burden, but emotionally, I was mortally wounded. Nothing in my life prepared me for the pain of his leaving a second time. For almost a week after he left I was unable to function. I refused to get out of bed. Ed and Jaime would check on me and I would assure them I was okay and just had the flu. Ed understood. He would try to talk about it, but I couldn't put my feelings into words. They were bigger than words. Not sharing my feelings allowed me some containment, for I felt I would surely die if I began to express my grief. But, as with any grieving process, the time came when

I had to move forward and begin to glue together the pieces of my heart.

Almost immediately Carl and Martha engaged in old habit patterns. They made plans for the weekends when Jay was to be with us, making it increasingly difficult for us to see Jay, always having some reason that appeared justified, at least on the surface. To argue and fight would aggravate the situation and increase the ugliness and pain for Jay.

I attempted to console myself by entertaining thoughts about Jay's impending adulthood. He would soon be graduating from high school and gaining independence. With some added years and maturity he would, hopefully, be able to sort out the truth of the situation. I held tightly to memories of better times. I hoped he knew that I loved him with every cell of my being. At the same time I felt hopeless about changing the course of his life, imposed by his decision to live with his father and Martha.

If the events of my life were displayed in a quilt, there would be areas of lightness filled with bright colors, and other patches of darkness chained together. When something wonderful happened, it seemed to be a harbinger of additional good. When something horrendous happened, it was like a magnet, attracting more problems.

Jay's leaving was the first in a series of negative events. Our business and the church began experiencing trying times. Jaime's schooling left a lot to be desired. My volunteer activities were plagued with people aimed at dissolving several worthwhile projects, including attempts to close a camp that served the special needs population. Challenges seemed abundant in almost every area of our lives. The only stability and solace I could depend on were my relationships with Ed and Jaime.

Bob and Cindy, the couple from church, asked us to join them on a spiritual retreat. It would be held at Serpent's Mound, an ancient Indian burial ground in the shape of a serpent, in southern Ohio. We needed a break from the normal routine, and this afforded us the opportunity to use our motor home, which had rarely been out of storage since our marriage. The process of packing for the three day trip generated an enhanced enthusiasm for life in general.

God created the perfect day for our trip. It was sunny, but not hot, and the glow of the sun poured out of a cloudless sky. Hundreds of people joined together, circling the length of the serpent, from the tail to its head, a distance close to a quarter mile. One could not escape the feeling of being in the presence of those who lay beneath our feet under the swollen mounds of earth. We shared a deep sense of peace and well-being; we were energized and renewed.

As the sun dipped below the horizon, we sat around the campfire sipping wine, and swapping stories and memories of other special moments. The time at Serpent Mound wrapped around us like a cloak of peace and quiet joy, soothing our minds and nurturing our souls. On the last night, lulled by the fire and the warmth of the wine and companionship of friends, Ed breathed a sigh of contentment and said, "I'd like to do this full time."

Bob retorted, "Why don't you?"

Ed looked at me, smiled and nodded, "Maybe we will."

It wasn't the first time Ed and I had entertained the idea. On many mornings, getting ready for work, we would tease each other with the statement, "Do we own the business or does it own us?"

The banter was followed by lofty ideas of retirement. With the recent business dilemmas that phrase had been used more frequently. It hadn't been more than a month ago when Ed, feeling particularly frustrated, had said, "Why don't we sell everything, climb into the motor home, and travel?"

I laughed, "No reason I can think of, let me know when you're ready."

Now when Ed looked at me across the glow and sparks of the camp fire, there was an unspoken exchange that relayed volumes. We couldn't talk about it in front of Bob and Cindy. They were church members and such a decision would likely have a negative impact on the church. But I knew a shift had taken place. It was part of the entire spiritual experience of the retreat.

On the drive home Ed was quiet as I chatted with Bob and Cindy. Nothing more was said about changing our lives, but the idea hung in the air between Ed and me. When we arrived home, cleaning out the motor home and unpacking had to wait, a church board meeting took precedence. Quick showers and fresh clothes made us feel presentable. Driving to the church Ed turned to me and said, "Well, what do you think? Should we do it? Are you willing to sell everything and travel full time? We could head toward California."

I teased Ed many times about getting "California eyes." It normally happened when he was sitting quietly. He would lay his book aside and stare into space. He tried valiantly to adjust to Ohio and the Midwestern lifestyle, but it was obvious he missed California. Listening to his description of California gave new belief to it being the promised land.

Everything in our lives had become so topsy-turvy, I was ready for a change. I heard myself say, "It's okay with me."

"Really?"

"Really."

"Should we tell them at the board meeting and give notice?"

"I guess so. How soon do you think we can sell everything and be ready to go?"

"Let's plan for two months. I'll give them a sixty-day notice."

"Okay."

"Are you sure?"

"Yeah...yes, I am. I don't understand it, but I am sure."

Ed opened the door to the church and nodded for me to enter. As I stepped into the church I heard him mutter under his breath, "Showtime." We gave our sixty-day notice that night and began to make plans to travel fulltime.

Family and friends were shocked. Not terribly surprising, it was a shock to us as well. In sixty days we had sold our business, lined up new ministerial candidates for the church, and sold our home and almost everything in it. What we didn't sell, we gave away.

In preparation for the trip, we took the motor home in for service. We had not left the service counter when a woman approached us, "I noticed you just brought a Holiday Rambler in for service. You wouldn't be interested in looking at one that is a little larger, would you?"

The idea of getting a larger motor home intrigued both of us. Ed and I had talked many times about the potential difficulties of traveling with Jaime and living together in one room, but in the past we had dismissed our concerns. Now we were on a mission and were not about to allow a little discomfort to stop us. However, now we were presented with the possibility of expansion. It appeared as part of a series of events about to happen. Since making our decision, it was as though we had jumped into a rapidly moving river and the waters were providing for us – all our needs were being met. The new motor home was part of the movement.

The saleswoman led the way toward a Holiday Rambler that looked new. Doubts began to set in about looking at a new motor home. It would be outrageously expensive and we had just made the decision to give up our income in order to follow our dream. The saleswoman sensed our hesitation and seemed to intuit the underlying reason, "This was just brought in this morning by a man who barely used it. It looks new, but it's five years old."

We fell in love with it. There was a separate bedroom and all the amenities of home. We signed the papers and left with our new motor home. Sitting behind the wheel, Ed grinned as he shook his head, "Certainly didn't plan to do this today."

"No, but then I've done a lot of things I never planned since meeting you – being a minister's wife, a business owner, a mother to three teenagers. Now this – selling everything and getting ready to travel fulltime – shoot, buying this motor home for the trip is the most logical thing we've done together."

"The timing does seem to be incredible."

"It was meant to be. I'm sure of it."

"Any doubts? I don't just mean the motor home."

I hesitated before answering. I hadn't planned to tell him, but the timing was right. "I had something odd happen the other night at church that ended any lingering doubts."

When I didn't speak for a couple minutes, Ed encouraged me to continue, "Well?"

"I didn't plan to share it because it's so weird. I was in the kitchen after prayer group and had some doubts cross my mind. Then I heard a voice, but there was no one else in the kitchen." I paused again.

"And...the voice said what?"

"I have to tell you Ed, that I never heard voices before. It spooked me out. The voice said, 'Be gone by December or Ed will be dead.'"

"Whoa! If I didn't have enough reason before, that convinced me."

"It convinced me too. Like I said, I never heard a disembodied voice before. It was loud and it was clear. Any doubts I had disappeared."

That was how we made our decision and prepared for our trip. Jaime's school made sounds of woe, but we were empowered with spirit and decided nothing and no one would deter us.

Jaime was especially excited about going to Hollywood. She was sure this was her chance of a lifetime, her opportunity to make her dreams come true. She was going to be a movie star. Jaime told everyone that she was going on a "big vacation."

— VI —

California Dreamin'

Life is either an adventure or nothing at all.
~Helen Keller

On the Road

When the time came to say good-bye to our many friends and to Jay, it was much more difficult that I thought it would be. My feelings were intense and mixed, happy and sad, eager and yet fearful, hopeful and remorseful. Sorting through possessions and figuring out what to do with everything seemed like the perfect metaphor for my internal world. I knew this was right for us. We were enthusiastic and excited. But, to leave our beautiful home and friends, and especially Jay, was excruciatingly painful. Emotions ruled. In the midst of a torrent of tears I thought we might need a boat to survive the flood.

As we left the city limits an aura of calm replaced the frenzy of the past sixty days. The reality of our sojourn began. Ed prayed out loud, blessing our new home on wheels and the trip ahead. I checked on Jaime, who was at the table with a Word Search puzzle book, "How are you?"

"I happy. Fun time."

Her simple words spoke volumes. I looked around the interior of our new home. The people who design motor homes should share their expertise with architects of residential structures. Every possible essential had been packed into this compact space of approximately three hundred square feet. I learned how to pack from reading every book I could find about full-time traveling. Those who went before us were wonderful resources. I was amazed to learn how many people were full-timers. We had a traveling home, and wherever we stopped was our current address. When another motor home joined us on the road I felt as if we were modern day pioneers, heading west. I was sure my emotions were being orchestrated by the gypsy in my soul.

Leaving behind the fast pace, high stress, and difficult business pressures of our previous life felt peculiar, but exhilarating. The structure of our days changed drastically. Deciding what road to take, when to start and stop, and where to stay were the only major decisions we had to consider each day. Adjusting to the ease of this lifestyle was like falling into a large soft feather bed. Everything about it was comforting and healing.

In the midst of one such reverie, I commented to Ed, "I love our new home. It feels like a magic carpet, taking us into a new dimension."

Ed chuckled, "Everything about this has been somewhat magical. There's no doubt we've been guided."

"Hmm, I think we should name our new home. How about calling it God?"

"That's definitely not one of your better ideas."

"What? Naming it or calling it God?"

"You know what I mean. We need a magical name."

"God's not magical enough for you?"

He glanced at me and shook his head, "You're impossible."

"Yep, that's why I need all the help I can get. I like the idea of having a reminder about living in God. I think it's a great idea...maybe one of my best."

Ed had a way of ignoring me when he felt a conversation had gone as far as he wanted it to go. "How about Merlin? He was a powerful magician who could change lead into gold."

"Okay, if you don't like God... then Merlin it will be."

"You have such a way with words. When we stop we'll drink a toast and make it official." He grabbed the steering wheel and stretched his arms as if greeting a friend, "Merlin it is."

Merlin was good for everyone. Concerns about Jaime not adjusting quickly dissipated. She amused herself with puzzles, books, music, and one of her favorite pastimes, watching other people. Jaime became a self-appointed guide. When we arrived at a new campground and were busy with check-in and setting up, she would grab a map and walk the grounds. On her return she shared her knowledge by taking us on a guided tour and introducing us to all the special features of our new neighborhood. She often made friends with our new neighbors before we did.

I had made a decision before starting the trip not to stress about Jaime's education. I purchased workbooks on writing and math and several educational computer programs. We bought a book on American Sign Language and began to teach each other. Our forced close proximity to one another and constant interactions intermingled with a continuously changing environment which brought opportunities for learning that never would have occurred in any classroom.

Traveling together we had opportunities for closeness that few people experience in a lifetime. Sharing thoughts, dreams, and the joys of simple pleasures amused and amazed us. Sipping morning coffee, walking unfamiliar paths, watching sunrises and sunsets at ocean's edge, and sharing the warmth of a campfire under starry skies were only some of extraordinary "ordinary" events that brought great peace and happiness to our days.

Guided and Directed

The highway stretched before us, leading to our agreed-upon destination – California. We followed the road with the anticipation of children following a ribbon connected to a desired prize. We were on I-40 just past Flagstaff, Arizona, when Ed noted a sign alerting drivers for upcoming State Route 89, the turn off to Sedona.

He slowed down and commented, "I heard there was a pulpit opening up in the Sedona church. Would you like to check it out?"

"I've read about Sedona. It's supposed to be beautiful. There's nothing to stop us."

"Nothing, except we just started on our journey. I don't know what made me bring it up. Just seeing the sign reminded me."

"Maybe that's what all this was about."

"It would be very strange if we left everything expecting to travel fulltime only to find a different church within the first week."

The idea made me chuckle, "God works in mysterious ways. However, I'm going to let you make the calls to tell everyone."

"It's only a few miles detour to go there. We could do some sight seeing and talk with the ministers."

I let out a gasp as a strange sensation ran up my spine, and I pointed at the sky directly in front of us, "Oh, my God, Ed, look at that!"

Clouds developed in an otherwise clear blue sky. They were in the shape of an arrow and pointed west, straight ahead.

Ed slowed down immediately, "Can you find the camera? If I didn't see it myself, I wouldn't believe it."

I grabbed the camera and snapped the picture, "I got it!"

"Well, that's the clearest sign I've ever seen. I'm convinced. Sedona will have to wait for another time."

"Okay by me. We've been guided every step of the way, we better not ignore this. I think we should give thanks."

Ed yelled, "Thank you, God!" We all laughed as Merlin picked up speed and continued straight ahead to California. The cloud dissipated as quickly as it had appeared.

The only plan for our entire trip was to attend a church conference at Asilomar, a state conference center, near Monterey. Going there allowed us to begin our journey spending time with old friends and meeting new ones. The rustic beauty of Asilomar connected with something deep in my soul. The entire place was perched on the edge of the Pacific Ocean and nestled among giant pines. The sun shone brightly and filtered through the trees. The air was cool and dry. California was as remarkable as Ed had promised it would be.

We received a variety of reactions when we told people about our leap of faith adventure. People we hadn't met would ask, "Where are you from?" Our response was always, "Where are we today?" This led to discussions about being full-timers. Some were astounded, a few were impressed, and others were amused. Observing reactions became part of the fun of traveling.

After the conference we continued in a southerly direction stopping in Paso Robles, Cambria, and San Luis Obispo to visit friends. Pine trees gave way to the rolling mountains sprinkled with ancient oaks, gnarled with age. Our trip was punctuated with "oohs" and "aahs" at God's handiwork. He did an awesome job of decorating the landscape and painting the skies, using bright blue and white during the day and a full array of colors including purples, yellows, pinks, and reds at dusk.

We were appreciating the formation of puffy white cumulus clouds in an otherwise baby blue sky when the scenery suddenly changed. After climbing a slight grade on Hwy 101 and rounding a bend the ocean stretched out below us. It was like thousands of giant sparkling sapphires spread at the foot of the rich green carpeted hills. The splendor took my breath away.

"Oh, my! It's incredible." I was overwhelmed with an inner knowing, "We're going to live here. Let's stop."

"We haven't been on the road two weeks. Do you think I'm ready to settle? This isn't the only pretty place in California."

"We don't have to settle, but don't you want to see where you're going to live? See that land that sticks out into the ocean. We're going to live there."

Ed smiled, "All in due time. I want to reach Buellton before dinner."

I satisfied myself by finding the location on the map and placing a circle around Pismo Beach and the Central Coast.

"If you love this, I can't wait to show you Malibu."

"Is that where we will be spending Christmas?"

"Yep, I called Bryan and he'll be joining us there."

Ed was right about Malibu. The campground was at the edge of a cliff overlooking the ocean. The sunsets were consistently brilliant and breathtaking. Each evening we set our chairs around the campfire and look out at the vista of the ocean and watched as splashes of red were thrown against the pale purple-blue sky.

Jaime loved the beach. Daily we gathered blankets, packed a lunch, and spent most of our time being kissed by the sun. After arranging her blanket, Jaime would sit cross-legged meditating. Finished with her prayers, she walked the shore line in search of precious sea treasures. She insisted on keeping every shell since she felt they were answers to her prayers – her personal gifts from God.

At lunch she would share her sandwich with the gulls, which were ever present. After several days, she found their brazen insistence for more food to be intimidating. Although annoyed with the persistent cawing, Jaime seemed to enjoy the daily exchange and the ability to set limits. When the sharing was complete, she would hold up her hands to show she had no more food. Some would fly away, but those who stayed were sternly instructed to leave. She would stand with hands on her hips and stare them down. A few more would fly away. She would then yell at the stragglers, "No! No food. You go – now!" With that she would point to the sky and laugh as they took flight.

As Christmas drew near I hung garlands around the outside of Merlin and purchased lights to outline the windows. Decorations had to be limited. There was no room for a tree, so I did the best I could. Festive table clothes covered the tables, inside and out. This Christmas felt so different from the years of open houses, one reflection of the many changes in our lives.

Christmas morning I heard Jaime yell as she stepped out of the motor home. I thought she had been seriously injured and rushed to the door. In a million years I will never forget that moment and what awaited me outside. "Oh, wow! I don't believe it! Ed, come quick."

When he arrived at the door Jaime was bent over and attempting to scoop up enough snow to make a snowball.

Ed looked perplexed as he reached out his hand to feel the snow that was continuing to fall. "Snow? Snow in Malibu?"

We hugged as Jaime threw a small sprinkling of snow at us.

"God sure has a sense of humor. You brought me to California where you said, 'It's always warm.'" Remembering the previous cold snowy winters of the east, I smiled, "It really is a very nice Christmas present, isn't it?"

It remained cold at Malibu, so we decided to head farther south to San Diego. We did not find it any warmer there. They had their coldest weather since the 1890's. I scowled at hearing the upcoming weather report. The cold front set in and was expected to remain; with it came rain. We were not used to being confined inside Merlin. After three days, I shared with Ed that I felt like Jonah in the Whale. "It was okay at first, but they're predicting this will last for another week or two. We've gone as far south as we can and it still isn't warm. I was hoping to be warm this winter."

"Why don't we go to the desert? How about Phoenix or Mesa?"

"That's a great idea, my friend Carol lives in Mesa. I'd love to see her again. We could also visit the Living

Bible Center and International New Thought Alliance headquarters. Maybe I could complete my ministerial training there."

"Sounds like a plan. How soon can you be ready?"

"About as long as it takes you to unhook us. Jaime, get ready, we're going to leave within the hour."

Arizona offered a different landscape, hauntingly stark in comparison to California. And another huge difference – it was warm. The people we met were as welcoming as the warm weather, both at the Sun Life RV Park and the Living Bible Center. Everything about our new location felt right. The biggest decision each day was when to go to the pool. We gave thanks often for this peaceful and healing time.

The sun went from warm to hot in March. Ed talked frequently about heading back to California, but we decided to spend Easter with the church and our friends before leaving. We used the month of March to travel north and visit Sedona and Prescott where the weather was perfect. Jaime and I spent much of our time climbing the hills and rock formations.

At the Point of Rocks Campground in Prescott there was a peacock named George, a mascot and self-appointed alarm clock. Each morning he would stroll through the center of the park, spread his feathers and crow about every thirty feet. He repeated this routine in reverse every evening upon his return. His home was a tree at the end of the park, which kept him safe from predators. I never saw George drop feathers anywhere else, but he left several feathers for Jaime, who was one of his biggest fans.

We enjoyed the Prescott area so much that we stayed longer than expected and had to rush back to Mesa in time for Good Friday services. Rev. Lola Pauline Mays created a memorable Good Friday ceremony which lasted the entire day. Every hour one of the last seven statements of Jesus was featured. People in the congregation presented mini-lessons about the metaphysical interpretations of each statement, followed by music, discussion, and food. Rev Lola insisted any decent church meeting should have these basic ingredients: thought provoking ideas, music, camaraderie, and food. Good Friday was no exception.

Jaime was strangely quiet throughout the day. In the early afternoon she asked to go home, and although we didn't want to leave the ceremonies, we reluctantly granted her wish. As soon as we arrived home, she got sick. At first I thought it might be something she ate. Then I felt her; she was burning up. Two hours later she remained dreadfully ill and her fever continued to rise. I took her to the emergency room, where the doctor shocked me with his report. She had pneumonia. It didn't make sense. She had had pneumonia several times when she was younger, but this time she hadn't coughed or shown any of the normal signs. It was a virulent strain, spread by birds, which the doctors thought she may have contracted when we were in Prescott. She slipped into a semi-coma shortly after being admitted. Friends and family were called for prayer support.

Jaime had only been in the hospital a few hours when Ed started showing signs of contracting a respiratory infection. I begged him to go home and take care of himself. I didn't want him to end up in the hospital. The hospital staff moved Jaime to a private room and provided a chair for me that reclined, and could be used as a bed. It was comfortable, but sleep had now become my enemy. I feared Jaime would not be alive when I woke up.

On the second day the nurses strongly encouraged me to go home. I refused to leave. In the middle of the night, I watched and listened to Jaime struggle for each breath. I was aware of the rising and falling of my own chest that coincided with a need to will her to follow suit. Hour after empty hour I monitored her breathing, which continued shallow and ragged.

She had been through so much already and repeatedly won battles against illness. She could do this. Was I doing everything I could to make sure she was getting the best care? Doubts invited guilt. Memories crept in about other times when Jaime had been ill.

With my eyes closed, her struggle for breath reminded me of her worst case of croup. She was four years old. Her barking cough shook the walls. The doctor assured me it was okay and all we needed to do was turn on a hot shower and keep her in the bathroom until it cleared. After several hours of this routine, and with no change in her condition, I had called the doctor again. He said we should continue. After several more hours, we looked like prunes and her cough wasn't better. Exhaustion won and we'd fallen into restless sleep, intermittently jarred awake by Jaime's cough. Sleep helped more than anything else, and Jaime's coughing steadily subsided. She recovered from the ordeal within several days.

Later I learned that a hot shower should only be used for short periods of time. It was a miracle she hadn't died. Each time I thought about that night I felt bad, knowing I had not done everything I could. I should have ignored the doctor and taken Jaime to the emergency room. This time I brought her to the emergency room. She was receiving excellent care, and I tried assuring myself, if she didn't die then, she wouldn't die now.

Was there anything else I could do to help her? I held her hand, closed my eyes, and another memory flashed before me with amazing clarity. I saw her covered with chicken-pox. She was only five when it happened. It was two days before Thanksgiving. She had just recovered from several weeks of being ill with pneumonia. I thought she could return to school the following Monday. We were looking forward to celebrating the Holiday.

It had been a rough time for us. As a working single mother, finding care for a sick child was almost impossible. Doing it for three weeks had been excruciating. My heart sank when I saw her covered with red dots on her chest. Throughout the day and into the night the dots had spread exponentially until there wasn't a half inch any place on her body without a pox mark. I called the doctor, who assured me it was okay.

She lay lifeless and moaned. Her fever spiked. I knew if I called the doctor again he would tell me, "Stop worrying. All kids get chicken pox. She'll be fine." I went to a medical book and looked at the symptoms. It read to call the doctor if the child has fever that rises above 102, has a severe cough or trouble breathing, an area of rash that becomes red, warm, swollen, or sore, a severe headache, unusually drowsy, trouble looking at bright lights, difficulty walking, seems confused, or has a stiff neck. With book in hand, I called the doctor's office again. This time I was prepared and asked the receptionist to write down all of Jaime's symptoms. I then read the list from the book. She placed me on hold to consult with the doctor. While she was gone, I asked for forgiveness for stretching the truth about some of the symptoms. I felt I received God's nod of approval when the receptionist returned and told us to come in immediately.

I wrapped Jaime in a blanket and carried her to the car. When we arrived at the doctor's office I carried her again from the car into the doctor's office. She was far too large and heavy to be carried, but a mother finds amazing strength when she needs to do something for her child.

I was struggling to open the door at the doctor's office when another mother with her child came out. She held the door open and as we slipped by, the blanket fell from Jaime's face revealing eyes that were nearly swollen shut and skin completely covered with sores. The child who was coming out of the building, quickly grabbed his mother's hand and yelled, "Look, Mommy, a monster!"

Poor Jaime. Her eyes just lifted and looked at me, begging for relief. We walked to the desk and as soon as the receptionist saw Jaime, she jumped up, ran to the door and rushed us past the other children and parents who had been waiting. Dr. Smith's eyes enlarged when he walked in. He looked at Jaime and said, "Wow! You really do have chicken pox."

Examining her, he checked her hands, the soles of her feet, her ears and in her mouth. Stepping back, he shook his head, "I've been practicing for fifteen years and I've never seen anything like this. She has pox as far down her throat as I can see. I'm glad you brought her in." He gently touched Jaime and reassured her, "We're going to help."

Too weak to respond in her normal enthusiastic manner, she half-smiled and said "You good." If I hadn't gotten the list of symptoms out of the book, the doctor never would have seen her.

Now, my attention returned to the hospital room and I looked at Jaime lying in the bed and listened for the rasping noise that announced another hard-won breath. I wondered if I should leave the hospital and try to get a book on pneumonia to convince the doctors of the seriousness of her situation. But Jaime was already in the hospital. All the doctors and nurses were aware and attentive. What more could be done? I closed my eyes and prayed.

The third day, Carol came to visit and insisted I eat something. We went to the cafeteria and within minutes of eating I got violently ill and lost control of all my bodily functions. Carol escorted me to the ER where I was treated. Nothing they did helped. My body was caught in repeated convulsions, although I never lost consciousness. Finally, a young doctor came in and instructed me to go home. He stressed the fact that my body was exhausted and it needed rest and help to rebalance itself. He insisted Carol stop on the way home and purchase some Gatorade. It seemed like an odd recommendation. He assured me it was necessary to balance electrolytes.

Much to my amazement, after four treatments five minutes apart, each consisting of two teaspoons of Gatorade, the internal spasms stopped. I was then able to sleep for several hours. As soon as I woke up, I returned to my vigil at the hospital.

In the afternoon of the fourth day I was praying, with eyes closed, when I heard the door open and turned to see a nurse entering. Just then I heard Jaime say, "A black face. I like that." Any other time, I might have been embarrassed. But her odd greeting let me know she was awake and had won the battle.

Good naturedly, the African-American nurse laughed, "What a nice surprise! Look who's awake! Welcome back." She walked to the bed and touched Jaime's face, "I like this face."

The death sentence had been lifted. I cried with relief. Seeing her awake and responsive was better than winning any lottery. Jaime's recovery seemed slow. The doctors kept her in the hospital for another week. While Jaime was recovering in the hospital, Ed continued his journey to wellness. As his health and strength returned our conversations shifted to plans for leaving. Our time in the desert was complete, I'd finished the ministerial course work and had been ordained.

The day after Jaime's release, we packed and left Arizona, fleeing like the Hounds of Hell were at our heels. I was incredibly relieved to leave behind fears of illness and death. When we crossed the California state line we let out a cheer and broke into song, "California here we come, right back where we started from..." It provided some illusory and imaginary safety.

We agreed before leaving Arizona to return to the Central Coast, the area I circled on the map the first time we traveled there. The return trip was slow and leisurely. Detours were made to see places that intrigued us and to visit friends. The cold weather was gone and it was replaced by sunny days with perfect temperatures. When we pulled Merlin into Pismo Coast Village, we fell in love with the surroundings. Large trees created a canopy to the entrance and the dunes provided protection from the winds. The fresh ocean air was palpable.

Immediately after hooking up, Jaime insisted on showing us around the park. Most of all she was thrilled to walk across a dune and find the ocean, where we would spend an enormous amount of time during our stay. Jaime's days were filled again with morning meditations on the beach and searching for star fish, conch shells, sand dollars, and other treasures left by the sea.

The idea of leaving paradise held no appeal. The days turned into weeks and weeks into months. Our decision to settle came as suddenly and easily as the decision to travel. As soon as we made the commitment to make this area our home, we found a three bedroom ranch style home with an open floor plan. It was perfect for us including having stone fireplace, a Jacuzzi in the back yard, and delightful fruit trees.

Return to School

When I enrolled Jaime in school, the woman at the office frowned with disapproval upon learning Jaime had not been in school because we were traveling. "We'll have to test her to see how much she lost over the past year."

For some reason, school personnel seem to treat everyone, even parents, as children, or at least that's the impression given when entering a school facility and interacting with staff, teachers, and other officials. I prepared myself for the upcoming reprimands when we met to review Jaime's test results. To avoid further negative evaluation, Jaime's outfit was chosen with care, her hair was perfect, and her expectant face as shiny and bright as the morning sun. The school psychologist who had conducted the testing entered the room with file in hand, "The director, Mr. Stevens, is going to join us." He opened his folder and began shuffling papers.

My mind raced to flash-backs of past meetings. At least I didn't have to wait long for Mr. Stevens to arrive. He entered the room with a big smile and outstretched hand, "Welcome to California."

I was aware of monitoring everything and feeling reserved and somewhat wary to his friendliness. We shook hands, "Thank you. It's nice to meet you."

He was tall and impressive. He took immediate command of the room and, after introductions, he asked for the file which held copies of Jaime's school records in Ohio and the results of the testing. Everyone was silent as we waited while he flipped through the papers, occasionally pausing to examine some piece of information. He pulled out several sheets and laid them on the table. He looked at Jaime, "Well, young lady, you are impressive."

I felt my neck muscles tighten and my head straighten in surprise at this opening line, "Really?"

Not known for false modesty, Jaime smiled and nodded her head, "Yes." She looked at me with a grin that expressed some inner knowing.

Mr. Stevens' handsome face broke into a full smile. He was obviously amused, "Yes, really. She did an amazing job." He pushed a paper across the table. "You can see here that in the past year her reading improved by three years and her math by two and half. We are always looking for ways to improve our school system and I asked to meet you today because I'd like to know what you did to help her to improve so much."

Thoughts of all the easy days with no agendas replayed in my mind, "I'm not sure what to tell you. Very honestly, we've been traveling and I didn't stress education. I decided not to worry about it."

He pushed back away from the table and relaxed in his chair. "So all we have to do is buy motor homes and have everyone travel."

"That might get expensive – you certainly would have a lot of people moving here to take advantage of your program." I paused before continuing, "Again, I'm not sure what to tell you. We did purchase Jaime a computer with educational programs, but I can't imagine those things improving Jaime to the degree her tests indicate."

Jaime spoke up, "I tell, Mom."

"Okay, Jaime." I didn't realize she had been tracking the conversation.

She sat up as tall as she could in her chair and leaned forward. She placed her folded hands in front of her, like a mini-executive ready to address staff. "I work computer. I do map. I read book and paper. I do puzzles. I sign." She then raised her arms in front of her and with hand turned out and index fingers pointed toward each other, she alternated index fingers, rotating them toward herself, demonstrating the symbol for sign language.

Mr. Stevens nodded his head and smiled, "I'm impressed. You're an exceptional young lady."

Once again, Jaime was in full agreement, nodding her head and smiling.

I reached out and patted her arm. I wanted to jump for joy and give her high fives and hugs and kisses. The pride bubbled up inside me, making me want to giggle, not just for what she had just done, but for who she was. I realized she had done all of those things without anyone asking or making her do them. Yes, we had purchased Jaime her own computer with educational programs. But when we stopped at used books stores along the way, she would pick up a supply of children's books. I also remembered how she would get information from the counters of the RV offices and ask for help to understand some of the words. Ed and I were constantly in close proximity and provided attention much of the time. Apparently, her education blossomed in the casual, no stress environment.

I didn't expect the next comment from Mr. Stevens. "With Jaime doing so well, we thought she might like to be mainstreamed into regular education classes."

"No!" The response was louder than I would have wanted, but this was totally unexpected. I came prepared to be chastised for not doing enough for Jaime. Then felt elated at the results of the testing. The heightened feelings of pride crashed at his suggestion. Fears of past failed attempts when Jaime was in regular education flooded back – painful memories of Jaime's daily torment and tears. "I'm sorry. I didn't mean to be so forceful. It's just that we tried mainstreaming and it was a disaster."

"Well, this is a different school system and…"

"Mr. Stevens, I don't mean to be rude, but I will keep Jaime out of school rather than have her mainstreamed. One of the reasons she did well this past year was because she didn't have stress. I know Jaime and won't agree to her being placed in regular education classes."

"Interesting…most parents with special needs kids fight to have them participate in mainstreaming, and you're telling me that under no circumstances will you agree to have Jaime in that program?"

I nodded my head, this time in more control, "That's right. I don't care what other parents do. I believe mainstreaming can be great for some kids, but not Jaime. I know what's right for her. At most, I'll consider having her enrolled in one regular education class. If she does okay with that, I'll approve another. But fulltime mainstreaming, absolutely not."

I could tell he was debating about continuing his agenda. As he looked into my eyes, he must have sensed the level of commitment ran deep – too deep to challenge. He made the right decision and let it rest.

Jaime enjoyed being back in school. Her teacher, Jackie Gonzales, reminded me of Miss Needle. They tried a mainstreaming class and within a month took her out of it and focused on independent living skills. When she was seventeen they found a job for her in the community at a print shop. Jaime learned to ride the bus to and from work. She met a lot of people walking to and from the bus, riding the bus, and working in a public place. We would go shopping and someone always greeted her by name. She came to know more people in the neighborhood that I did.

Love – Pure Love

On New Year's Day the following year Ed received a call from a church in the near-by town of Santa Maria. The call came as an answer to our daily prayer, "Where would You have us go? What would You have us do? What would You have us say and to whom?" Ed and I were offered the position as their ministers. We accepted their proposal after a short discussion, deciding it was another gentle nudge by the hand of God.

When I looked at a map I laughed our loud. Santa Maria was in the center of the land mass that I pointed to the first time we drove through Pismo. It was exactly where I said we would live.

Jaime's teacher, Ms. Gonzalez, did not want Jaime to leave. Even the director, Mr. Stevens, called to say, "I can't believe you are leaving. You know we consider Jaime to be a star in our program. Is there anything we can do to convince you to allow her to stay?"

"You and Ms. Gonzalez are making it difficult to leave, but we really feel we need to do this. It's been a great year and I can't thank you enough for everything you've done. Your program has helped Jaime in many ways. You even made it possible for her to fulfill a lifelong dream of going to a school prom."

I immediately experienced a flashback of watching Jaime greet her date, Johnny, who had arrived in a tuxedo. As they walked hand in hand toward Ms. Gonzalez, who was waiting by her car, I was sure for Jaime it was no ordinary vehicle, it was her chariot. Her bright smile and parade wave as they'd driven off was etched in my mind's eye. Thinking about all the good things that had happened to Jaime since we moved to Arroyo Grande made it hard to say good-bye.

All the literature indicated that people with Down Syndrome do not accept change easily. Jaime always seemed to be an exception. She thrived on change. However, leaving Arroyo Grande and Ms. Gonzalez was a textbook experience. Jaime cycled through all the stages of grief. Initially, she engaged in denial, refusing to believe we were moving. She was angry, sad, and even attempted to bargain with me. She was inconsolable.

I began to wonder if this had been the right decision. But, the decision had been made and there was no turning back. Santa Maria High School was large – much larger than any school Jaime had attended. Jaime cried as we pulled into the parking lot, "No, Mom. No." I smiled and said with a great deal more reassurance than I felt, "It'll be okay, Jaime. I know you miss Ms. Gonzalez, but I'm sure you'll like it here."

Quickly after meeting her new teacher, Julie Fromme, I knew it really would be okay. Julie's energy was contagious. She enthusiastically introduced Jaime to classmates, having all of them, in turn, tell Jaime something about themselves. They planned a welcoming party. Jaime felt accepted and wanted.

My only concern was a reaction to some of Julie's ambitious promises. When she learned that Jaime had worked at a print shop in Arroyo Grande, she said they would find her a similar job. When Jaime said, "I like Richard Simmons," Julie said they would find a jazzercise class for her. I wondered if Julie's visions for Jaime might not be a little lofty. My fears were groundless. Julie found Jaime a job at a local print shop and enrolled her in a jazzercise class at a nearby parks and recreation center. The world was a happy place again. Jaime would often arrive home from school, hug me, and say, "I so happy. School good. Fun place."

At the church Jaime was a special blessing. She never had to be asked twice when preparing for the church services. No matter what needed to be done, she thought of herself as God's helper and did everything she could think of to make others comfortable. One of the jobs she liked best was handing out programs and greeting people. We had been at the church several months when Irma Zellar approached me. Irma, a founding member, could be somewhat intimidating. She was totally proper, immaculately groomed, and fully in command of every situation. At board meetings she made it known that the church would collapse without her. I felt honored and relieved that she was supportive of Ed's and my being the ministers.

Irma cleared her throat, "We need to talk about something – a problem."

"Certainly, Irma. Should I get Ed?" I was hoping for reinforcement.

"No, I don't think that's necessary. This is something you need to take care of."

"Well, I'd be happy to help you, what is it?" I broke a cardinal rule. Never offer help until you know what the other person wants.

"It's Jaime. You can not continue to allow her to greet people. Decent people will not attend church if she is the first one they meet."

Stunned and speechless I just stared at her. Words could not express what I was thinking, and if they did, I wouldn't be allowed to repeat them in church. Stammering, I attempted to speak, but couldn't find my voice.

"I knew this would be difficult, but you really must do something about it before we frighten new people away and – well, even some members who have been here forever may leave."

Standing mute, it took what seemed to be an eternity for me to answer, "Uh...I'll talk with Ed."

Although the scenario ran through my mind many times, I didn't talk with Ed for a couple days. I was dumbfounded and hurt and angry. Finally, I knew I'd better say something before he was caught off guard by Irma talking to him. "I've been thinking about something that happened on Sunday. We need to talk."

"Okay, talk." His glib retort showed he had no idea about what I was about to say.

"Irma spoke with me Sunday about Jaime."

"What about Jaime?"

"She doesn't want her to greet people. She said she'll frighten off new people – all the "decent" ones."

"Nonsense! I'll bet she was kidding."

"There was nothing teasing about what she said. She was totally serious. She even implied she and some other long-time members might leave. I've never been so upset; I haven't been able to talk about it. She wasn't joking." I started to cry.

Ed's arm encircled me. "It's okay. Let me deal with this."

"What are you going to do? You know how powerful she is. We need her support. I can't stand the idea of telling Jaime she can't greet people. I certainly can't tell her Irma thinks she's scary."

"I'll handle it. The church is a place everyone is welcome – but they have to decide if they want to come or not. Jaime's an important member; she does a lot of work. She hasn't done anything wrong. I've seen her greeting people and I haven't seen anyone have a negative reaction. This is Irma's problem; she'll have to deal with it."

"But how? How can you tell her 'no'? We're so new."

"How? No. That's how."

"She won't like that. Maybe we could be at the door with Jaime."

"You know how things are Sunday morning, getting ready for service. That's not practical, but you've given me an idea. I'm going to offer the job of greeter to Irma. If she's not willing, then that's the end of the subject."

Ed handled the situation with Irma. I never asked anything more about it. Irma didn't volunteer to be a greeter. Jaime continued to meet everyone as they came in, sometimes with a second person from the congregation. I still have trouble with the idea that adults would come to church with such trepidation and closed hearts.

We had a saying, "People shouldn't come to church to find God, they should come to share Him." If there were exceptions to that, Irma was one of them. She left the church within a few months. It was a good change for everyone. A phrase came to mind that I used on my door when I was in business: Some bless us by coming and some bless us by going. Irma blessed us.

The church grew and attracted families with children. Judy, a dedicated member who was a first grade teacher, accepted the position of Director of

Sunday School. Jaime found another job she totally enjoyed – helping with the children. She actively participated in the class, so I thought something was wrong when Judy waited for me after church. "Linda, one of the best parts of teaching Sunday school is working with Jaime. I have to share what happened today."

"Do I need to sit down?"

"Absolutely not. It was wonderful. I presented a lesson on a balanced life and the importance of doing both work and fun activities. The children then gave examples of the work they do and what they like to do. I always include Jaime in our questions and answers."

Thinking of Jaime's ability to confuse most any story, I asked, "You're sure I want to hear this?"

Judy's eyes brightened and she smiled before continuing, "The children talked about liking toys and games and TV shows. Jaime was last and waited quietly and patiently. I thought she might be having a hard time thinking of something, but she surprised all of us. When it was her turn she only had one word to share: 'Love.' Isn't that incredible? What she enjoys is love!"

I looked at Jaime, who was busy picking up hymnals and cleaning up after the service. The room blurred as my eyes filled with happy tears, "She is love...pure love. Sometimes people hear that I have a daughter with Down Syndrome and they say they're sorry. They have no idea how lucky I am to have her as my daughter."

— VII —

Destiny

He has achieved success who has lived well, laughed often, and loved much.

~Bessie Stanley

Special Olympics

Jaime participated in Special Olympics from the time she was eight years old. She tried a number of events, but didn't find her true calling until we settled in Santa Maria.

When she was only nine months old she learned to swim during a "Mommy and Me" swim class. Those skills developed over the years and improved significantly when we traveled and swam almost every day. Columbus didn't have a Special Olympic swim team, so the opportunity to swim competitively did not open up until the move to California.

Jaime attended every swim meet and loved bringing home "the gold." She was one of the few Special Olympians that did the butterfly stroke. This particular stroke tests the best swimmers due to its demand for perfection and its rigorous nature. Jaime loved the challenge. At times she won because no one else entered for the butterfly stroke. Her claim to fame was winning a first place ribbon from the state competition in the butterfly stroke. It wasn't her speed that won, but her exactness and attention to detail. All the other swimmers were eliminated because they did not perform the stroke correctly.

After one of the out-of-town swim meets Jaime refused to attend swim practice. The first week I thought she wasn't feeling well, but after the second week I decided to investigate. I learned about an incident which had happened on the way to her last swim meet. One of the swimmers, a teenage boy with autism, raged and kicked the window out of the van. The police were called to restrain him and it obviously left a lasting impression on Jaime. Her refusal to swim reminded me of a similar situation that happened after she saw the movie, "Jaws." It took many patient hours of going to the pool every day during our trip to slowly desensitize her to a fear that sharks might be lurking around in swimming pools waiting to taste unsuspecting swimmers.

This time, no amount of coaxing was sufficient to convince her to return to competitive swimming. Discussing something with Jaime when she doesn't agree is like trying to encourage someone who is short to become tall. She does not get angry, although she may look at you in a manner that makes you wonder if you are seriously demented. At times, she puts on headphones to shut out uninvited comments and at other times she simply ignores whoever delivers unwanted news. She turns into a statue – a four foot eight inch statue – a perfect representation of an immoveable force. When Jaime makes her mind up about something, no one and no thing changes it – not even the desire for blue ribbons. She never returned to competitive swimming.

I encouraged Jaime to try out for other Special Olympic sporting events. She finally agreed to try the bowling team. This provided opportunities for her to meet a different group of people. When I picked her up the first day at bowling, she was beaming. A nice looking, well groomed, young man with Down Syndrome was carrying her bowling bag. I was somewhat surprised because Jaime had never been attracted to someone with Down Syndrome before.

Searching for Love

From an early age, Jaime was fascinated by love: people in love, dating, dancing, hugging, kissing, and weddings. One of her favorite drama reenactments was falling in love, receiving a proposal of marriage and having a big wedding. One enormously frustrating aspect of raising a child with special needs is the lack of information about what to do when their hormones start moaning.

Jaime's romantic fantasies became a reality when she was twenty and entertained her first boyfriend. Paul was tall, dark, and handsome. They met at a social club dance. When he came to our house for the first time I was surprised. His vocabulary was extensive and he was able to converse on a number of subjects. I wondered how he fit into a group with developmental disabilities. I then learned he had a severe seizure disorder, which made him eligible for special services. His intellectual impairments were minimal. When he came to visit Jaime they would watch movies, play video games, go on walks, and talk. I was happy she'd found someone to share time with who was such a nice young man.

Paul visited two to three times a week for several months. Jaime was excited when he invited her to a barbeque at his parents' home. Upon their return, he dropped Jaime off and kissed her on the cheek. He never returned. Jaime called him, but he didn't call back. Jaime was confused and cried – a lot. I finally called his mother, "I feel odd making this call, but I'm trying to understand what happened to Paul. He seems to be avoiding Jaime since the barbeque. Did something happen that I should know about?"

She hesitated before saying, "That was our first chance to meet Jaime. Paul talked so much about her... but, he never mentioned her... disability. His cousins and other family members gave him a bad time. We don't think it's a good relationship. I'm sorry." She hung up before I could respond.

I stood motionless. My grip tightened around the phone. I wanted to scream at her and her family, "How could you be so stupid!?" But, there was no one there to yell at. I reached out to redial the number. Instead, I just sat the phone back in its cradle, sat down, and cried. A million scenarios ran through my mind about what would be the best way to handle this: everything from driving Jaime to their house and demanding they tell her why Paul was avoiding her, to telling Jaime Paul had a new girlfriend, or even that Paul had died. I knew she would most likely see him again, so the last solution wouldn't work. What could I do? When

Jaime saw him, I knew she would ask and I was afraid of what he would say to her in public. Why didn't God give me a crystal ball so I would know the right thing to do? It seemed like it was the least He could do at a time like this. I prayed for Divine intervention, but when I opened my eyes the world remained the same and I still had no clue about what to say to Jaime.

I decided to blame it on his mother; after all it was her family. Throughout history mothers have been blamed for the majority of the world's ills, so why not add this to the list of horrible things mothers have done. It gave me an opportunity to talk with Jaime about Down's Syndrome. Jaime never saw herself as having any type of disability, so this prejudice was nearly impossible for her to comprehend.

I did the best I could and started with, "Jaime, I talked with Paul's mother. She said she doesn't want Paul to see you anymore."

Her eyes grew large and misty, "Why?"

"I think it has to do with you having Down's Syndrome. She said you seem like a nice girl, but she wants Paul to be with someone who has no problems."

"I okay. No problem."

This wasn't going well, "No, not that type of problem. It is about you not being as smart as Paul."

"My brain?" This was how Jaime understood Down's Syndrome. Her brain did not work the same as other people's, which made it harder for her to learn.

I nodded and reached out to hug her. As she placed her head on my chest I rubbed her head and whispered to her, "I love your brain. I wouldn't want you to be any other way."

When Jaime stopped sobbing, she pulled away, looked up at me and said, "She stupid."

I laughed, "Yes, very stupid."

"I find new boyfriend."

"That would be a good idea."

Nothing more was said about Paul and I no longer heard crying behind her closed bedroom door.

A Sad Affair

Within three months after breaking up with Paul, Jaime brought Jeremy home. He was tall, blonde, and handsome. She was attracted to good looks. Jeremy always seemed sad and one day he shared that he was having trouble with his medications. It was my opportunity to satisfy my curiosity, "Oh, what medication do you take?"

"Depakote, Wellbutrin, Risperdal, Tenex, Buspar, and," he paused for a long time, "there are some others. I can't remember all of them."

I worked as a behavior analyst and knew if someone took all of these medications, they had severe problems. "Uh, wow, I can see why you might be concerned. What are your meds for?"

"I'm schizophrenic... paranoid schizophrenia."

I felt like Paul's mother and wanted to turn to Jaime and yell, "Run, Jaime, run!" But I felt Jaime had been wrongly judged by a label and there was nothing Jeremy had done to cause concern. It was a learning experience for me. I prided myself on my level of tolerance and lack of prejudice. Schizophrenia, especially paranoid schizophrenia, was different than

Down's Syndrome. I heard people with this disorder could be dangerous if they had a psychotic break, and he wouldn't be on so many medications if he had no behavioral problems. My fears grew. I talked with Jaime and tried to gently convince her that Jeremy might not be the right person for her. She didn't believe me and they continued to see each other.

She and Jeremy came home hand in hand, "Mom, we talk."

"Okay, what do you want to talk about?"

She beamed at Jeremy, "We get married."

I swallowed hard, but the lump remained in my throat, "Wha... , what?"

Jeremy, who seldom smiled, grinned, "Jaime asked me to marry her and I said yes."

"Oh, wow! This is a surprise."

"I have to move out of the group home anyway, so it seems like a good time for us to move in together."

"What happened that you have to move out of the group home?"

"I got in a fight – a couple fights. I don't like it there anyway."

The possibility of violence was at the core of my concern about Jaime seeing Jeremy. Now they were discussing marriage. It was more than I could handle.

My work as a behavior analyst gave me an inside track to many agencies and I knew almost everyone in our community who worked in the field of disabilities. I decided to call Roxanne, the case manager who worked with Jeremy and Jaime. I had known her for years and knew she would help me through this current predicament.

"Hi, Roxanne, this is Linda."

"I thought I might be hearing from you."

"Oh? Does that mean that everyone has heard about Jaime and Jeremy wanting to get married?"

"Not everyone. Jeremy called me to ask for help. But good news travels fast, so I expect this should travel like lightening."

"Uh... I didn't exactly think of this as good news."

Roxanne laughed, "I thought that might be the case."

"Roxanne, please, you have to help me with this. This can't happen."

"Why?"

"It's not right. They aren't ready." I didn't want to admit my prejudice against Jeremy.

Roxanne was not sympathetic, "What do you mean they're not ready? They've been dating for more than a year."

"But I'm worried about him and his temper. He told me about getting into fights."

"He never hurt her and I don't think he would."

"You don't think he would, but you don't know."

"No, I don't. But I've been his case worker for a long time and I think Jaime is the best thing that has happened to Jeremy."

"What about Jaime?"

"I think he is good to her. They are good for each other."

There was a long silence as I tried gathering my thoughts for what to say next. I had known Roxanne for years, not only because she had been Jaime's case worker, but my behavioral work was contracted through the regional center, and I had done a lot of work with many of Roxanne's clients. Through my behavioral work I had become friends with many of the case workers. Roxanne was one of those people I knew personally through work, and socially. I couldn't believe what I was hearing her say.

"Linda, I'm going to do everything I can to help them find a place to live."

I lost it and almost screamed at her, "What? I don't believe this! I call with concerns about Jaime's future safety and you're telling me that you are going to help her live out this fantasy and put her in a position of not being safe? Neither of them has ever lived on their own. I won't allow it!"

"Calm down, Linda. Normal people often get married and move out of their parents' home when they haven't lived alone before."

"But Jaime and Jeremy are not normal. And he has a history of being violent."

"I know it's hard to accept, but they're adults and have a right to be together. I will fight you on this one."

"You'll what?"

"I'm going to support Jaime and Jeremy. If you try to fight this, you will be the one who loses. I will contact the attorney who advocates for our clients."

I was being threatened with legal action if I tried to interfere! At first I didn't believe Roxanne. I made four more phone calls to other people who worked in the system and who I knew might have some influence. They all repeated Roxanne's message. Jaime and Jeremy were adults, and since they had not been legally conserved, they could do what they wanted to do. I checked out the possibility of filing for a conservatorship for Jaime. Those efforts met with the same fate. I was told Jaime was too high functioning. No judge would approve a conservatorship and if I tried, the advocate attorney would file a counter petition.

I thought about buying a new motor home and packing up and leaving town in the middle of the night. Finally I decided if I couldn't reason with the system, I would use some of my mother's wiles with Jaime and Jeremy. Ed and I invited Jeremy over to discuss the situation.

I began the conversation, "So, you two still want to get married?"

They nodded their head. Just the way they looked at each other told me they guessed my agenda. Their hands and arms were interlaced. They were holding on to each other for dear life. Jaime had the look of determination that announced without words that she was not going to change her mind.

So, I started to outline every possible catastrophe I could think of, "Have you two thought about where you are going to live?"

Jeremy nodded and he whispered, "Roxanne is going to find us a place."

"Is Roxanne going to pay your bills? I drew up some numbers here and want to share them with you." They leaned forward as I pulled out a tablet with numbers written all over it. "Here, look, just the basics, rent, gas, electric, water, phone, and food will cost more than the two of you make."

Jeremy said, "We'll work more hours. I already talked to the people at work about that."

"Do you see that you don't have enough for food?"

Jeremy again quietly commented, "I have friends who are married. They work where I do, they make it."

"You might just make it, but there won't be any extra money to do anything fun. You won't be able to go to a movie or even rent a video."

They looked at each other, "We'll be okay." Jaime and Jeremy remained firm in their resolve.

There seemed to be no solution until Ed intervened. He never liked Jeremy. Not because of his disability, but because Jeremy lacked some basic hygiene skills and smoked constantly. Ed spoke up, making an appeal that reached deep into ancient archetypes, "Jeremy, man to man. You know Jaime has special needs and she needs a man who can take care of himself. Before I can approve of you two getting married, I'd like you to show that you're capable of taking care of her. To do that you have to first show you can take care of yourself. So, why don't you move to your own place and if you are able to do that for a year then we will help you two. Is that fair?"

Jaime and Jeremy went off to talk and came back in agreement. Surprisingly, they would postpone their plans. Jeremy found a studio apartment at a place where they catered to the special needs population by providing meals as part of the monthly fee. Jaime was happy with the new arrangement and marriage was only brought up once in a while.

Jeremy continued to have problems controlling his temper. After a fight with another employee and then his boss, he lost his job at a sheltered workshop. He was smart enough to know working would be one of our requirements for marriage, but try as he might, was never able to maintain a job.

They continued to see each other for another two years before Jeremy broke up with Jaime. He found another girlfriend. It ended as quickly as it had begun.

Ed and I tried to hide our relief and yet I felt so guilty at the same time.

Jaime was heart-broken; nothing we did or said could console her. For several months we listened to sounds from her bedroom of melancholy music and crying that often gave way to sobs. I wondered if she would ever heal and if we had done the right thing.

New Love

Watching Jaime walk out of the bowling alley smiling and holding the hand of a young man, I sensed the sad days of mourning Jeremy were passing. Jaime smiled brightly as she introduced him, "Hi Mom," she nodded toward the man standing next to her. "This Mark. He need ride. Okay?"

"Hi, Mark." Past experiences taught me to verify everything Jaime told me. "Do you want a ride?"

He replied clearly and with intention, "Hello. Yes, Ma'am. That would be nice."

Mark was immaculately groomed and extremely polite. This was the type of person we had been wanting for Jaime. On the ride home he said, "I've had my eye on Jaime for a long time, but I knew she had a boyfriend, so I didn't say anything to her until today."

"Well, I'm glad you spoke up."

They looked at each other and laughed. He said, "Actually, she said something first."

Jaime was pleased with herself as she explained, "I ask, 'You have girlfriend?' He say, 'No.' I say, 'You want one?'"

Mark reached over and hugged her, "So, she is now my girlfriend."

They both laughed. It was obvious they were pleased with their new arrangement. Life seemed so effortless, unambiguous, and uncomplicated for them. My initial response was embarrassment when Jaime shared how she approached Mark. I wanted to tell her it wasn't appropriate. But, who was I to judge? It worked for her and for them. I then thought it might be a kinder world if everyone could be as direct as Jaime with their wants and needs.

Jaime and Mark began courting immediately and saw each other frequently, sharing many of the same interests and totally enjoying each other's company. I was amazed at their ability to use individual strengths to overcome each other's weaknesses. Jaime had difficulty with speech and relied on Mark to translate for her when someone couldn't understand what she was saying. It was amazing – Mark never seemed to have trouble interpreting what she wanted to say.

Mark was socially adept, but extremely anxious. When they went to new places, he became fearful. Jaime would hold his hand, assure him everything was okay, and help him remain calm in the most difficult of circumstances. They were perfect together.

Over the next two years they were inseparable. When they weren't together, they were on the phone.

Getting Serious

I was surprised when Mark's mother, Irene Garrison, called. I had never met her. When Jaime and Mark needed transportation either I would drive or Sam, Mark's father, would take them. If they were going to be late, or if there was a question about whether or not Jaime could do something, his father would call. However, after two years I thought it was a good thing to meet his mother, even if it was only by phone.

After introducing herself, Irene said, "I just want to tell you how much we like Jaime and how happy we are that she is Mark's girlfriend."

"I feel the same way. They have been good for each other and make each other so happy."

"I'm glad you feel that way. I wanted to let you know ahead of time that Mark purchased Jaime a ring for Christmas and will be asking her to marry him."

I was speechless; her comment brought back memories of Jeremy.

Not noticing my silence she said, "You're okay with that aren't you?"

Working to maintain a normal voice tone and inflection I responded, "Well, there could be slight problem. Another boy asked Jaime to marry him and Ed demanded at that time that anyone who wants to marry Jaime must be able to take care of himself. In order to show that he's capable, Ed wants the man to live on his own for a year."

Irene laughed as she said, "That's not a problem. Mark lived on his own when we lived in Michigan."

"How soon does Mark expect to get married?"

"We didn't really talk about it, but I think it's probably going to be at least a year."

I gave a sigh of relief. A year would allow me enough time to plan and be able to end some of the activities I was involved in. Right now my life was ultra busy, I felt stretched to the max. I was holding down a full time job, in addition to church work, and teaching classes at the local college and university.

When Christmas arrived, Jaime was ecstatic with her engagement ring, a pretty little solitaire diamond. The newly engaged couple bubbled with joy. It was easy to join in their excitement. I watched Jaime with awe. When she set her mind to something, she always achieved it. From the time she was five years old she played wedding. Why did I ever doubt it would happen?

Overcoming Obstacles

I began checking with Social Security and other agencies to find out what impact getting married would have on their resources. There were several major problems: Initially, Social Security told me she would lose her disability status. I checked with an advocate attorney and learned that was not true, but her monthly check would decrease significantly. Another major roadblock was insurance. Jaime's father was mandated by court to maintain private health insurance through his work. If she married, she would lose that. And housing was a major issue; where would they live?

I was talking with a friend about these concerns and she suggested Jaime and Mark just live together rather than get married. They could avoid all the potential pitfalls, except for housing. We discussed it. Mark was visibly upset as he explained how he felt, "I love Jaime, but I can't just live with her without us being married. God wouldn't like that."

I knew he attended an evangelical church that professed some basic strict tenets of right and wrong. I thought about his perspective before sharing another idea, "Why don't we have a commitment ceremony at our church. It won't be an official wedding, but you two can make a commitment to love each other. The ceremony would be like a wedding and you could say vows in front of your families, friends, and God, that you won't be with anyone else."

Jaime's brow furrowed, "No marry? No pretty dress?"

"No, you could still dress up. We would write vows. It will look like a wedding, but we won't have a minister doing the ceremony. You won't sign papers saying you are married. That way you can live together with God's blessing, still be single for the government so you won't lose money, and you'll be able to afford to live together. What do you think?"

Mark and Jaime asked to talk privately. I prayed as they talked and with God's help, they agreed. When I approached Mark's parents with the idea, I didn't expect there would be any problem. Mark shared several times that his parents didn't go to his church and were nonbelievers. I expected they would be relieved that Jaime and Mark would not lose any money, which meant they could make it financially. Irene's response surprised me, "I don't like it. If they aren't married Jaime could just leave him. The first time they have a fight, she'll be gone. I don't think it will work."

"Jaime isn't easily swayed. When she makes a decision, she sticks by it. Plus, they've had disagreements before. They've been together almost two years. For them, this will be a wedding. It just won't be formal with the government."

"I don't know."

"If their Social Security is cut, they won't have enough money to live together."

"I don't think that's true."

"Irene, I would like to come to your home and bring the paperwork the advocate attorney gave me. Can I come over right now?"

I had never been to Mark's home. It was a pretty place in a quiet neighborhood. Sam greeted me at the door neatly groomed. He was a good looking man of moderate height and slim build. Mark must have gotten his fashion sense from his Dad as both of them always looked like they stepped out of a fashion magazine. I wasn't prepared for meeting Irene. She wore a tent-type housedress and her grey hair was fashioned into what seemed like a helmet. Even though she smiled, she had the look of someone who spent too many days being unhappy.

She was friendly enough and Sam offered to get us something to drink before we started looking at all the documents and figures I had brought. After reviewing the paperwork, she conceded, "Well, I guess it is true." She paused for a long time before saying, "As long as they see this as a life-long commitment, I guess it will be okay."

With everyone in agreement, we moved forward with the idea of a commitment ceremony. In March Irene began searching for an apartment for Mark and Jaime. I was relieved when she reported back that there was nothing they could afford. After all, she had said it would be a year and I was somewhat confused about why she was looking now.

I was happy when she told me Jaime and Mark's new caseworker, Mary, suggested they apply with Section 8. That process would take a year to eighteen months. Much to everyone's surprise, within two months of applying, Section 8 housing was given extra money and what normally took a year to eighteen months was reduced to four months. Irene immediately resumed apartment hunting for Section 8 properties, and soon found an ideal place only three blocks from us.

Once the apartment was available, we had to move ahead quickly with plans for the ceremony. I seemed to have generated a list of commitments longer than my time and energy, but I started sleeping less and squeezing in the extra demands in preparation for the big event. A close church friend of our family, Judy, agreed to do the ceremony. The vows were fashioned after a traditional wedding, without finalizing them by using the statement, "With the power vested in me by the state of California I now pronounce you man and wife." Any reference to husband and wife was changed by inserting their names and the word marriage was replaced with the word commitment.

Everything proceeded with relative ease. Jaime and Mark decided it should be a formal affair. I worried about finding the right dress for Jaime. It was nothing less than a miracle when we found a simple princess style white dress that was perfect for her short stocky frame.

Jaime and I talked about who she might want as her maid of honor. She said she was going to ask Cherrie, a long-time friend. Cherrie often looked after Jaime when we went out of town. She escorted Jaime and Mark on numerous activities and outings. They both knew her and liked her. It was a good choice, and was one less thing I had to think about. I called Cherrie and asked her. She was delighted.

The next weekend when Jaime returned from spending a day at Mark's, she told me she had asked Mark's sister, Annie, to be her maid of honor. Annie lived in Los Angeles. Jaime barely knew her. I never met her. When I asked why she changed her mind, Jaime told me, "Irene said."

"Irene? Irene asked you to have Annie be maid of honor?"

Jaime nodded and her face began to cloud. She sensed my unhappiness. Recently, unhappy feelings seemed to crop up frequently after the mention of Irene's name. I was stunned into silence as I thought about Irene doing this. She arranged for someone

Jaime barely knew to replace our family friend as her maid of honor. Even though Annie was Mark's sister, it just seemed over the top. I took a deep breath and decided I was going to call Irene and let her know this couldn't happen when Jaime touch my arm. "You okay, Mom?" She was worried. I did not want her to worry. I wanted her to be happy. This was to be a happy time.

"Are you okay with Annie being the maid of honor?"

She nodded, still observing my reaction.

"Okay, this is your special time. I want you to do whatever will make you happy."

Jaime threw her arms around me, "Thank you. I love you."

I smelled the freshness of her hair and hugged her tighter, "I love you, too. All I want is for you to be happy."

Good and Bad

Jaime and Mark needed furniture. Mark asked his father Sam to make them a bedroom set. Sam was an excellent wood craftsman. Even though he was retired, he must have worked night and day to finish it on time. It was magnificent. The dresser had simple lines, but was expertly made and was finished in a light oak. The bed was a true work of art with posts and carved scrolls on the headboard.

Irene and Sam spent days searching through second hand stores to find just the right furniture for the rest of the apartment. They made a lot of decisions without asking Jaime or checking with me. However, the furniture was attractive and they hadn't asked for money, so I ignored being left out of the decision-making. With so many other commitments in my life, I appreciated their involvement and dedication.

I know I could not have done it without them. It was a wildly busy time in my life. My schedule was beyond demanding. Although I had resigned from my part time work as a behavior analyst, I worked fulltime as a therapist at a mental health clinic and part-time as the minister at our church. I taught two classes at a local university in the evenings and I was studying for a national behavior analyst certification – a demanding test that was only given once a year.

Many times I thought if only Mark and Jaime could wait, I would have been far more available to assist with all the preparations. When I broached the idea of waiting until after the first of the year, Irene reminded me how difficult it had been to find the right apartment and assured me she and Sam were enjoying what they were doing and had everything under control.

I was surprised to receive a phone call from Irene at my work. I had a number of things on my mind and a client waiting to see me. "Hi, Linda, this is Irene. Sorry to bother you at work. Do you have a minute?"

"Normally it would be fine, but I do have someone waiting to see me."

"Well, I'm busy, too, so this will only take minute. I want to have a shower for Jaime."

"I thought I would do that."

"You're always so busy, let me do this. I have a lot of family who will come and you don't have any family in the area."

Her curt summary of my family hurt, but it was true. Just then my supervisor stuck his head in the door, "Linda, you have a client waiting."

I bit my lip and said, "Okay, Irene. Can I call you when I get home so we can discuss details?"

"I'm busy tonight. I want to have it three weeks from now on Thursday night."

The supervisor was waving his hand, trying to get me to end the call.

"Okay, that's fine. I will call you in a couple days to discuss details."

"Fine." The line went dead.

Just before bed I mentioned the upcoming shower to Ed. He said, "Did you forget you teach Thursday nights?"

"Oh darn! I'll have to call her and ask her to change the date. That's the night of the final exam."

"Can't you shift and have it on another night?"

I pondered the idea. "No, it's impossible. It's a unique class, with each night building on the previous one. There is no way to rearrange that class."

"How about meeting on another night?"

"You know the classes are planned a year in advance. There are other classes given each night, I couldn't get a classroom and even if I could, many students take several classes. Neither the school nor the students would allow it." I sat down and held my head which was throbbing from too little sleep over several months and too many conflicting demands.

Ed wanted to help, wanted to find a solution, "If it's final night, why not have someone sit in for you?"

I shook my head and started to cry, "I can't. Normally that would not be a problem, but this final is being done with oral presentations. The students have been preparing for them the entire semester. I have to be there to grade. No one else would know what they are talking about. No one else can do it. And I can't even cut them short – it wouldn't be fair to the students who have worked so hard and are paying a healthy amount of money for this experience."

"Sounds like you don't have any choice except to ask her to reschedule it."

I nodded my hurting head, "It's too late to call tonight; I'll do it tomorrow."

The next day was extremely busy, starting with one of my clients, a young boy, who was suicidal. It took me out of my office for most of the day. The call to Irene slipped my mind.

I remembered the next morning and called shortly after eight o'clock. She never failed to surprise me and her response was no exception, "I can't change it. It's already planned. Perhaps you can come after class."

"Irene, it's a four hour class. It would take me at least a half hour to get to your home. The earliest I could be there would be 9:30."

"Well, I guess you'll miss it."

I made several more attempts to get Irene to understand the predicament I was in. She would not budge.

When the conversation ended I sat for several minutes attempting to get my bearings. How could I be angry at someone who had done so much for Jaime? But, I was. And I was hurt. This was a shower to honor my daughter and I wouldn't be able to be there. I called back, "Irene, I'd be glad to send out new invitations, if that's the problem."

"No, I haven't sent them out. I just made plans with my daughter who's coming in from LA. I don't want to ask her to change her plans."

"I'd be happy to call her and explain what happened."

"You will not." Her tone turned dark and threatening.

"But it will mean that I won't be able to be there."

She was immoveable, "That's your decision."

"It isn't a choice. I have to be at class for oral presentations; no one else can grade those for me. We won't finish until at least nine."

"I made my plans. Sorry, I can't change them because of you. You were the one who forgot."

"Yes, I did and I am truly sorry." It was obvious she wasn't going to change her plans. I admitted defeat, "I'll tell you what. I appreciate you having this shower. I understand you have family that will be attending. I'll just have another one for Jaime's friends from VTC, where she works."

"I already invited everyone from VTC."

"You what? I thought you said you hadn't sent out invitations."

"I called her boss today and found out who her friends are and wrote the invitations. They'll go out tomorrow. I also checked with Jaime about the people she wanted to invite."

"Irene, I was serious about being willing to purchase new invitations and I will fill them out and send them."

"And I was serious that the date has been set. There's really nothing more to talk about. I hope you change your mind and can make it." A click let me know she was finished talking.

Change my mind? Change my mind! It wasn't about changing my mind. She was being impossible. I was being shut out of my own daughter's wedding shower. Yet, there were no alternatives. I was trapped. I never felt more like a failure as a mother than I did at that moment.

Keep Praying

Planning the ceremony was taking every extra moment I had, plus some I didn't. I decided that getting into a bigger fight with Irene about the time and date of the shower would only aggravate the situation. I talked with Jaime and explained things as best I could. It wasn't easy, since I didn't understand it. I blamed it on me and my lack of organization that happened with an overly full schedule. Memories of past injustices with her father nearly overloaded my circuits.

Jaime handled it better than I did. She reassured me it was, "Okay." There was no indication of her being angry or upset with me in any way. I counted my blessings that I had raised such a beautiful daughter. To make it up to her, I decided I would dedicate myself to making the ceremony and reception as stunning and memorable as anyone could.

Jaime chose to carry a single red rose instead of the traditional bouquet. Using that theme, I created invitations with paper that had a single red rose on the side. Jaime helped with stuffing the envelopes and preparing them for mailing. She squealed and jumped up and down over and over again when she learned that her brother, Jay, was planning to come from Ohio. She hoped her father would also be there to walk her down the aisle. I called Carl several times to keep him informed of Jaime's plans. Each time he shared he would check with his wife.

Carl called when he got his invitation, "This is not a real wedding, why are you pretending it is?" He didn't wait for an answer, "I can't believe you're allowing them to move in together without being married. I don't approve of it. You can tell Jaime we won't be there. We won't be part of this in any way."

I attempted to help him understand. I explained all the reasons. He wouldn't budge. I had to break the news to Jaime. I told her they were busy. It was so hard to do. First her mother didn't come to her shower and now her father wasn't attending her commitment ceremony – the only wedding she would ever have. I was angry at him, but I hadn't gotten over being angry at myself for missing the shower. Struggling with my own personal guilt and self-irritation, I found it difficult to be too judgmental of him.

One of Jaime's favorite jobs is collecting the mail. She brought a letter to me. The envelope was addressed to her; it was from her father. She asked me to read it to her. I should have read it first, but no training would have prepared me for what was in that letter.

"Dear Jaime, We are not coming to your ceremony and we want you to know the reason. You are not getting married. What you are doing is bad. It is evil to live with someone if you are not married. If you do this you will be evil. Do not call. We do not want to talk to someone who is evil. Dad"

Jaime ran to her room and slammed the door. I could hear her sobs. I wanted to run to her, but I could not move. I was frozen into a pillar of pain. I heard another great primal sob and realized it came from me. The letter burned in my hand. I crumpled the paper and threw it across the room. I couldn't console Jaime when I was in such personal turmoil. I wanted to pick up the phone and tell Carl exactly who was evil. He'd hit an all time low. I wanted to catch a plane and go to Ohio and kill him. It was the only relief I had, envisioning ways to make him suffer.

How could he call this woman-child, who never expressed anything except unconditional love, evil? His self-righteousness turned his heart to stone and deafened him. There was no chance of reasoning with him. He would never hear a thing I said. So, I went to Jaime and held her.

As I held her to me and stroked her hair, I said, "Daddy is wrong. He is wrong. You are love." I kept repeating those words, "You are love."

As her sobs decreased, she looked at me with eyes red and swollen, "Why, Mom?" Then a smaller plaintive plea, "Why?" as she once again buried her head in my chest.

I shook my head, "I don't know. I think he may be sick and it's making him think in a bad way. Maybe someday God will help him to see that he was wrong."

She gave a great sigh; it must have made sense to her. She looked at me again and said, "We pray – Daddy be okay."

She was asking me to pray for him. I prayed with her. It was the most difficult prayer I ever prayed.

The Ceremony

Irene made arrangements with Jaime for Mark's sister, Annie, to pick her up early on the day of the ceremony. Irene insisted, saying it was the right thing to do. The bridesmaid should help Jaime get ready. I was disappointed, since I wanted to be the one with Jaime, but once again I rationalized that I had a lot of work to do getting things prepared and ready for the reception. I kept reminding myself of how badly I messed up with the shower and decided not to object.

When Annie came to the door to pick Jaime up, I was a little apprehensive. This would be our first meeting. Surprisingly, she looked nothing like her mother, but like a younger version of me. She was slender with long dark curly hair. She was bubbly and bright and obviously excited for Jaime. She shared how much she liked Jaime and I felt good about her being the maid of honor.

When they arrived at the church and Jaime stepped out of the car, I thought my heart would burst. She was radiant in her white wedding dress, with just a touch of makeup to accent her china doll complexion. Mark was smiling and handsome in his tux. Neither of them seemed to be the least bit nervous. Mark chose his cousin, David, to be best man. Jaime and Mark loved David. He seemed to enjoy being with them and had taken them to several events over the past year, including the Rose Parade.

Jay flew in from Ohio. Jaime was thrilled to have her "big brother" escort her down the aisle on this most important day.

The sky was baby blue speckled with tufts of white cloud. The temperature was seventy–five. It was a perfect September day. All was right in the world.

The ceremony was simple and yet exquisite, accented with several songs chosen by Jaime and Mark: *The Wedding Song (There is Love), You Are the Wind Beneath My Wings, The Rose, You Got a Friend, and You are the Sunshine of My Life.*

As our dear friend, Judy, conducted the ceremony, the gentleness of her voice carried immense caring throughout the delivery of the commitment vows. Friends and family watched with eyes glistening, passing tissues around to catch the overflow of emotions. The only thing missing, which kept it from being the ideal wedding, was the omission of the normal "wedding" vows, which had purposely been avoided.

After they made a promise to love and be faithful to each other, Jaime and Mark chose to end with a candle ceremony. Judy spoke the words with much poignancy:

"Our gracious heavenly Father, who has given the supreme gift of love to Thy children, we thank You for bringing these two together. We thank Thee for all those who have loved and supported Jaime and Mark and for all the years of shared joy and happiness. We thank Thee for the love that has bound these two hearts together.

As Jaime and Mark enter upon the privileges and joys of life's most holy relationship and begin together the great adventure of building a Christian home, we thank Thee for all the hopes that make the future bright. Teach them the fine art of living together unselfishly, that, loving and being loved, blessing and being blessed, they may find their love ever filled with a deeper harmony as they learn more perfectly to share it throughout the years.

Each life is like a flame that burns brightly, lit from the One, the Eternal Divine fire. Today Jaime and Mark have made a decision to share their life, to share their light. To represent that decision they now will light a candle from the same light, the same candle, in honor of the fact that they will share their lights and their lives with God."

Judy stopped while Jaime and Mark each took an end candle from a candelabrum that held three candles, and together they lit the third, the middle candle.

Judy then continued,

"Our gracious heavenly Father, help them to keep the candles of faith and prayer always burning in their home. Be their Guest at every meal, their Guide in every plan, and their Guardian in all that they do.

No one can know what the future holds. All who love them ask that You, Oh Lord, will be a constant presence in their lives as they love, honor, and cherish each other always. May they be forever faithful and patient with each other, and may their lives be filled with joy and the home which they have established will become a haven of blessing and a place of peace."

Judy nodded at Jaime and Mark. They blew out their individual candles and placed them back in the candle holder.

There were two roses lying on the altar. Each picked up a rose and walked to the other's mother. Mark gave me his rose and Jaime gave hers to Irene. As Mark and I hugged he said, "I love you."

I whispered back, "I love you."

I looked across the aisle and noticed that Irene was not hugging Jaime and she didn't respond when Jaime told her she loved her. Jaime was oblivious as she hurried back to the center position at the altar. She turned to Mark, tugged on the sleeve of his tux and whispered loudly, "Now kiss."

Mark beamed as he turned to the friends and family in attendance and said, "I've been waiting for this." One more grin at his audience and he put his arms around Jaime and kissed her. Everyone cheered, except Irene. I couldn't imagine what was happening. She had been the one who pushed for them to be together.

Ed announced that he wanted everyone to join the happy couple for a reception at the Santa Maria Inn, a quaint old hotel noted for its warm ambiance. Ed and I had rented a deluxe suite which would serve as a place for the reception and for Jaime and Mark to use during their honeymoon.

As the guests were greeted, each told Jaime and Mark what a wonderful couple they were and expressed appreciation for the touching ceremony. A pianist was playing soft background music on a keyboard. The richness of the suite, the music, and the buffet collectively created a festive atmosphere. I could not have been more pleased with how things were turning out for Jaime on her special day.

In the midst of my reverie about how perfect everything was, a friend rushed up, grabbed my arm and urgently whispered, "You need to go and save your daughter from that crazy mother-in-law."

"What?"

"Right now. Don't ask questions. I'll tell you later. Hurry, they're in the bedroom. Get Jaime away from her."

Cindy was an attractive, petite, dark-haired pixie who had seen more trouble in her young life than most. She was not easily flustered. The intensity of her concern worried me and moved me into action. When I entered the bedroom I saw Irene sitting in a chair with Jaime standing in front of her. She stopped talking as soon as she saw me. Still not understanding, but following Cindy's instruction, I said, "Oh, there you are. Jaime, I need you for a minute."

Jaime turned to look at me, her eyes red and filled with tears. I decided to ask, "What's going on?"

Irene responded, "Nothing. She's just overwhelmed by the day, right Jaime?"

Jaime looked at her and nodded.

"Well, come and we'll get a cool cloth for your face. This is supposed to be a happy time." I gave Irene a look to emphasize there would be no more upsetting talks with Jaime.

It took Jaime ten minutes to get calm, but she wouldn't share anything about the conversation with Irene. After making sure Jaime was surrounded by friends and not near Irene, I found Cindy. She suggested we talk in the hall.

"Okay, Cindy, what in the world was going on? When I got into the room Jaime was crying, and it's taken me all this time to get her calm."

"Linda, there is something really wrong with that woman. She was horrible. She was telling Jaime she shouldn't talk with you now that she's married. Jaime should only listen to Mark and his family. She said you were no longer her mother and, honestly, I don't know what else she said because when I heard that I ran to find you."

"What? She told her I was not her mother? Are you sure you heard her correctly?"

"As sure as I am standing here. I heard her as clearly as I hear you right now."

"Maybe something was said before you heard them that would put it in context. Irene's been great with Jaime."

Cindy glared at me, "Believe what you will. Remember, I tried to warn you."

"Cindy, I really appreciate you coming to get me. There was obviously something happening, Jaime was tearful when I walked in. And she refused to tell me why she was crying. Jaime's always talked to me."

"See, I told you."

"Yes. I just don't know what to do about it right now."

"Go and knock Irene on her ass and tell her if she ever says anything like that again, you'll knock her out permanently."

I had to laugh. "Now that would make for a memorable day! I think I'll just hold it in my head right now and try to act as happy as I felt before this happened."

"I would say I'm sorry I told you, but I'm not. I wish you could have heard her. There was such a menacing tone in her voice. I think she's evil. I don't say that about many people, except my ex." She laughed lightly and gave me a sympathetic hug. "I'm afraid this does not bode well for the happy couple."

"I hope you're wrong. I'll talk with Jaime later. Thanks for everything. I know you wouldn't have come for me if you didn't believe it was important."

She nodded and we went back to the party. I tried to act as happy as Jaime and Mark. Looking at them together, hugging each other and radiating their love to everyone in the room, made me push the information about Irene to a dark corner in my mind. I thought I might address the situation with her after the guests left. That never happened, Irene and Sam left early.

— VIII —

Beginnings and Endings

Love does not begin and end the way we seem to think it does. Love is a battle, love is a war; love is a growing up.

~ *James A. Baldwin*

Home Sweet Home

Jaime and Mark enjoyed their stay at the hotel, but were excited to return to their apartment which Irene and Sam had set up for them. Many times I offered to help, but they insisted on taking care of it. When we brought Jaime and Mark home from the hotel, Jaime and I sorted through some of the gifts and began putting the kitchen items in the cupboards. Mark walked into the kitchen and stopped when he saw what we were doing. His face darkened, his voice raised, and his tone had an edge as he asked, "What are you doing?"

Shocked, I replied, "Putting the gifts away. Why?"

His voice was low and stern, "You better not mess up my mother's cupboards."

"What?"

"You better not mess up the cupboards. Don't move anything. She spent a long time fixing them."

"Mark, this is your home and Jaime's home. Jaime needs to be able to arrange the cupboards so things are convenient for her."

"You leave the cupboards alone."

Jaime chimed in, "Okay. It okay. No fight. You go, Mom."

I had just been told to leave. I felt stunned and unbalanced. My head was swimming with fears about this man who my daughter had just made a commitment to and who she would be living with. What in the heck was going on? I had never seen him act like this. My child, who was now a woman, had just asked me to leave. "Are you sure?"

Jaime smiled and nodded. I saw no fear within her. She went to Mark and hugged him, "We okay. We happy."

The drive home wasn't long enough to process everything that had taken place in a few short weeks. Irene had done several things that were odd and, in retrospect, they were now growing from odd to bothersome. I remembered her making arrangements for telephone service for Jaime and Mark. She hadn't consulted with me about it. When I heard what she had done, I called her, "Hi Irene. I heard you arranged for a phone at the apartment."

"Yes. And?"

"Well I didn't know if you knew that Jaime has her own phone number. The phone company found an easy number so it would be easy for Jaime to remember."

"And?"

"Well, I thought if it's okay I could call the phone company and make arrangements to have it transferred."

"I don't think that's a good idea."

Slightly stunned, I paused for a moment, "Oh. Why?"

"I think they should be starting with a number that belongs to both of them."

I paused for a moment, trying to decide how to continue. Should I argue with her? Would it do any good? I decided it wouldn't, "Okay. I just thought it might be easier with Jaime's old number."

"No, that's not a good idea. By the way, I ordered cable for Mark's television."

"What about Jaime's? It's my understanding that they want to have his TV in the living room and hers in the bedroom."

"Um. That's what Mark said, but I only ordered cable for his."

"I don't think they can pick up any stations without cable, so they'll need cable for both TVs."

"Okay, I'll talk with the man when he comes to install it."

"You may want to let them know ahead of time.

"I'll handle it, Linda." Her final comment still hung in the air when I heard the click from her hanging up.

I wondered why she responded this way. I didn't think anymore about it until I visited the apartment and saw Jaime's TV had no cable. I asked Mark, "I notice you got cable on your TV; do you know why they didn't hook up Jaime's TV?"

"My mom said it cost too much. It was five dollars more a month. Plus, Jaime should watch the same shows I watch. She doesn't need a separate TV."

I decided to call Irene and find out what happened, "Hi Irene, this is Linda. I just went to the apartment and noticed there was no TV cable for Jaime's TV.

"That's right I decided not to order it. They wanted five dollars a month for it."

"I thought we talked about it and you were going to do it?"

"I talked to the man and he said he thought she'll be able to pick up one or two stations. If not, she can order her own cable."

"That will mean another installation fee."

She ignored the comment and said the same words Mark used, "Jaime should watch the same shows as Mark, so she won't need her TV. By the way, I want you to give me Jaime's check book. I'm going to open up a joint account for them."

"I don't think that's a good idea. I want Jaime to keep her own bank account."

"That's outrageous. She needs to put her money in a joint account so I can pay their bills."

"No, remember, they have an independent living coach who will work with them to pay their bills. Toni said she'll help them to divide the bills so they can each pay some comparable bill or they can pay half of each bill."

"That makes no sense. Mark and Jaime should have one account"

"Okay, why don't you open an account for both of them and they can each put in whatever money is needed to pay bills. Then they can keep their own separate accounts."

"That's stupid!"

"I'm sorry you feel that way. I'm not willing to advise Jaime to put all of her money with Mark's."

"Why? How much does she have?"

Not liking the way the conversation was heading, I didn't answer. "I have to go now. I'll check on the cable." I remembered my hand shaking as I placed the phone back in its cradle.

As each event took place I made excuses for Irene's behaviors that were now collectively worrisome. My stomach felt like home for a pack of gremlins and a nauseous sensation burned in my throat. Pulling into the garage I parked the car and laid my head on the steering wheel and cried. What in the world had Jaime gotten herself into?

Adjustment

Over the next several weeks I called Jaime many times. She was always cheerful, but our conversations were short. I kept telling myself this was not unusual for her. Mark was the only one she ever talked to on the phone for more than a minute or two. Cindy's warning that Irene told Jaime not to talk with me kept playing over and over in my head. Why didn't Jaime ever call me? Why had all the phone calls been initiated by me? I shook my head, trying to shake the nagging, negative ideas out from the hidden recesses.

I decided to call Toni, the life skills coach, to obtain more input. She was seeing them every couple of days.

"Hi, Toni, I wondered if you could give me an update on how you think Jaime and Mark are doing?"

189

There was a long pause. This wasn't normal for Toni. More often than not, I had to ask her to slow down. She seemed to operate at the speed of light and was one of those people who had so much energy they were exhausting just to watch.

"Toni? Is something happening I should know about?"

"I was wondering how long it would be before you called."

"Because...?"

"There was some stuff that happened, but I think we've worked everything out."

"Like what?"

"Jaime hasn't said anything to you?"

"No, I call almost every day, but she is being very cryptic and doesn't say anything."

"Hmm...you might want to spend some time with her this weekend."

"Are you going to give me any clues?"

"Mark hasn't been going to work very much and he isn't doing his share of the work that had been agreed upon. He gets Jaime to do everything. And then there is the food situation."

"What about food?"

"Well, I helped Jaime put the new groceries away and Mark got upset that I put her groceries on his shelf."

"Oh, the cupboard thing."

"What cupboard thing?"

I told Toni about Mark's response to our putting the gifts away. "I'm getting worried Toni. I need you to tell me about anything odd that may be going on. I know Jaime's an adult, but in many ways she's still a child. There's been some other things that happened with Irene which bothered me. Can you just keep your eyes and ears open and let me know about anything out of the usual that goes on?"

"Okay." Toni seemed to understand, "I have to run; but I'll call if I catch wind of anything going on."

Everything seemed to settle down and Mark and Jaime reported being happy.

In fact, Mark called me to tell me they had gone to Section 8 to finalize their paperwork and the lady at the office was really happy when he told her they got married.

"You told her you got married?"

"Yes." He beamed.

This changed everything. We had gone through the commitment ceremony, carefully avoiding the words wedding, marriage, husband, and wife. Now he told a government official that they were married. I called Mark's Dad. He had gone with them to the Section 8 appointment. "Is it true that they told the worker at Section 8 they were married?"

He laughed, "Yeah. She made them resign all the papers using Mark's last name."

"Did you tell her that they are not married?"

"No, I didn't see that it was such a big deal."

"Not a big deal? Did you forget that it will affect their income and Jaime's insurance?"

"I don't think the government agencies talk. It won't make any difference."

What planet did this man come from? It was my daughter who had to resign all the papers with a

191

different last name and now he wanted to pretend it never happened? Jaime went through the trauma of being shunned by her father so she could maintain her single status. I was less sure than ever of their ability to remain together with the events of the last few weeks. But, they signed government documents saying they were married. It seemed the only thing to do was to have a private ceremony and make the marriage official.

Jaime and Mark's actual wedding took place quietly in their apartment. Jaime wore her wedding dress and Mark a suit. Our friend, Judy, who performed the commitment ceremony and her husband were the witnesses. The only other people present were Ed and I. Ed performed the wedding. Mark's parents refused to participate.

The next few weeks were peaceful and I began to believe everything would be okay. The initial rough spots were just the normal adjustments of two people changing their lives. It's not easy for two people to learn to live together when they have above average intelligence and are fully functioning. It was no wonder that Jaime and Mark struggled.

Then another call came from Toni, "You aren't going to believe what happened."

I sat down, knowing a warning from Toni meant something close to a major earthquake event. I knew I would not like what Toni was going to tell me.

"Linda, they took Mark's chair away."

She didn't need to tell me who 'they' were, but the news was shocking. "What? The blue one? It is like a security blanket for him."

"Did you know he slept in that chair?"

"No. You mean at night?"

"I mean every night. He told me he's always slept in that chair. He hasn't slept in a bed for years."

"What?! How odd. Why in the world would they take that away from him? Isn't there some law that he can make them bring it back? He's an adult."

"Apparently Irene found out that he was still sleeping in the chair and not in the bed with Jaime. So Irene had Sam take it away. She figures now Mark will have to sleep in the bed with Jaime."

"Call Mary, his case worker and let her know." I was sure she would intervene. "You have to let her know."

"I've done that. She says she's tried to reason with this mother about other things, but has had no luck in convincing her that what she's doing is detrimental to Mark and Jaime."

"What about the dad? Seems like he might be the reasonable one."

"Yes, but he does whatever mama wants him to do. Like taking the chair away."

"Do you know what they did with the chair?" I was thinking I could call and talk with Irene."

My heart sank as Toni shared, "Irene said they took it to the dump. Mark's devastated. I honestly don't know what to do."

"Okay, I'll call Mary to see if there is anything we might do."

It was discouraging. Mary had no ideas. After talking with her I just felt irritated, frustrated, and hopeless.

I called Jaime to invite them to dinner. She checked with Mark. He said they were going to his parent's for dinner. Once again, I was being shut out. Toni, their independent living aide; Cathleen, Jaime's supervisor at work; and Mary, her case worker, had become my ears and eyes. I didn't like what I was hearing or seeing. Jaime was becoming increasingly tired, but insisting she was okay.

Challenges

It was late November. I stopped by the apartment to take some leftovers that Jaime could easily heat and serve. Approaching the apartment I could hear Mark screaming and moaning. I ran the last few yards and pounded on the door. Jaime peaked out from a small crack before allowing the door to swing open. The apartment had been demolished. Mark was standing in the center of the living room shaking and crying. Jaime stood silent. Her face was blank. She appeared stunned. I quickly assessed what was going on and asked Jaime, "Are you okay?" She nodded.

"Did he hit you?" She shook her head.

Mark came to me bawling with his arms extended, "Help me, Linda, please, help me. I don't know what to do."

I put my arms around him and allowed him to cry. When he became silent and stopped shaking, I suggested we talk. He shook his head, "Can't do that."

"What happened that got you so upset?"

"My mom and dad. They don't understand."

"What did you fight about?"

He shook his head and looked at the floor, then began to sob again.

"Okay, Mark. You don't have to talk, but we have to clean this place up."

He nodded.

Broken glass was everywhere. I decided that would be the first thing to attend to. I assigned jobs to Jaime and Mark. They moved like zombies. No one talked as we picked up the big pieces of glass and other debris that had been thrown around the living room and kitchen. The furniture had not been put back into place and picture frames still hung lopsided on the walls when the doorbell rang. Jaime answered it. Mark's father stood at the door and quickly took in the amount of destruction.

He looked at me and asked, "What are you doing here?"

"I just stopped by to see Jaime and found them in the midst of this." I waved my arm at the apartment.

He looked at Jaime, "Did you call your mother?"

She shook her head.

I spoke up, "No, she didn't. And that concerns me."

"Don't worry, I have this under control. You can leave."

"It doesn't look under control. The place is still a mess. He's broken everything that's possible to break." I picked up an old pencil sharpener that had been my father's. It was broken beyond repair. I held it out. Now I felt the loss and personal assault against something that could not be replaced. "What is happening?"

"Sometimes Mark has trouble with his temper. He hasn't had a rage like this since we lived back East. I promise I will talk with him. We'll straighten the rest of this up."

I looked at Jaime. "I think you should come home for awhile." I was thinking, like forever.

She stood in place and looked at me.

"Just for a little while."

She shook her head.

"Let's go to the store."

She shook her head. She walked to Mark, put her arms around him, and said, "I love him. I stay."

It was clear I was being asked to leave. I offered to remain and finish cleaning. They all told me to go. I walked out the door. My feet belonged to someone else. My arms had not felt this empty since I left the hospital without taking Jaime home after her birth. Once again I was leaving her behind and for the life of me, I didn't know what else to do.

I talked with Ed about my concerns. I talked with Mary, Toni, and Cathleen. No one knew what to do. Jaime was an adult. She had the right to live wherever she wanted, with whomever she wanted. I thought about other mothers who knew their daughters were being abused. No matter how much a mother may love her adult child, there was no way to ensure their safety. When a child is an adult, the mother has no rights – even when that child has special needs.

I went to the phone a hundred times to call Irene and tell her...tell her what? That I was mad? That I would not allow this? I had no choice. I had to allow this. The thought made me angry and ill. I always set the phone down without dialing the number because I really didn't know what to say.

The next week I got a call from Irene as if nothing had happened. "We're going to Vegas for Christmas and I made arrangements to take Mark and Jaime."

"Did you check with Jaime's work? After the wedding they told her that she absolutely couldn't take any more time off until next year. Her boss was adamant about it."

"I already made arrangements. She'll have to tell them."

Jaime's work ethic is nearly heroic. I knew she loved Vegas, almost as much as Mark, but to go against a specific command given by her boss. This was a dilemma of epic proportions.

Unwanted Calls

Each time the phone rang it sent an electrical current through my nervous system. Every call seemed to bring increasingly awful news. They started with Jaime's boss, Cathleen, "Linda, I'm worried about Jaime. I had to tell her she could not take the time off to go to Las Vegas. I think you should check on her, she was pretty upset."

"Is there any way she could go?"

"No, there is a big push right now to have all the clients working when they are supposed to. She used up all her vacation."

I immediately called Jaime and asked how she was doing.

"Fine."

It was the only word she uttered. I waited. Nothing.

"Jaime, Cathleen just called and said you were upset."

"I okay."

I could hear Mark in the background, "Get off the phone."

She whispered, "I go now" and hung up.

There would be no sense in going to their home. It would aggravate Mark and make things worse. I called Cathleen back and let her know.

The next call came from Toni. "I think we got problems."

"You mean more than Mark destroying the apartment?"

"That was a shock wasn't it?"

"To say the least. And then I learned from Sam that Mark has a history of raging. He said something about it happening when he had his own apartment in Michigan."

"Oh, so they told you?"

"Yes, and I wasn't happy about his mother lying to me. I specifically asked her if he had trouble with his temper. She assured me he didn't."

Toni had known Jaime for years. She knew about Ed's mandate to Jeremy, that he had to live on his own for a full year before we would consider allowing Jaime to live with him. "Did Irene tell you Mark lived on his own?"

"Yes." There was a pause, a question hung in the air. I sensed there was more.

"I should have said something as soon as I learned."

"Learned what?"

"Mark never lived on his own."

"What?"

"He lived with a girl. It ended because they had horrible fights."

I sat down, trying to absorb this new information. It kept trying to escape as I denied it, "No. No. She said he lived alone. She said there was no history of aggression.... Oh, Toni... Oh shit." I held my head with my free hand, my favorite self-soothing habit. What else didn't I know? "Toni, do you know if he's hit her?" My stomach turned before Toni could respond.

In a slow thought-filled tone she said, "Not that I know of."

I breathed a sigh of relief. "Thank God." Then I thought, why did she hesitate for so long before answering? "Would you tell me?"

"Yes, I would."

"Why did you hesitate?"

"He's been rude and demanding toward Jaime in front of me, but I've never seen him hit her." After another short hesitation she continued, "On the other hand, I don't know what happens when I am not there. They've become really secretive. And now this whole business about Vegas. Did you know about Vegas?"

"Uh huh. Yep, but I don't know what in the hell to do about it."

"I think you should call Irene and tell her to back off."

My new close friend, frustration, quickly crept into my voice, "Like you think she would listen to me?

Have you tried talking with her? I don't think she would listen if God made a personal phone call to her."

"I know. I know. But, this is bad, Linda."

"What's happening that has you concerned?"

"Mark isn't working at all. He isn't taking care of himself. He just sits and does nothing. Jaime works – all the time. I think she is glad to get out of the house. When she gets home, she has to cook, clean, go to the store, do laundry, and I don't think she's sleeping much. It's been this way ever since they got married, but it got worse after they took that damned chair. And now this thing with Vegas. Why can't Jaime get time off?"

"I've talked with Irene, I've talked with Cathleen, and I tried talking with Jaime. She won't even talk with me about it. She won't talk with me at all lately. Between Irene and Mark, Jaime has pretty much shut me out. I tried calling her case worker, but she's new and doesn't seem to understand. She acts like I'm the trouble maker. Since she authorizes you to work with Jaime and Mark, maybe she would listen to you. Try calling Cathleen. Please. Toni – call anyone – call everyone. I am so worried, but for the first time in my life I am feeling truly helpless. It's like Jaime's in a prison and I can't get to her."

For a few seconds the phone was silent. I could feel Toni's aggravation. She called me to help and I was useless. I never felt so inept in my entire life. Odd. Here I was – the mother who was able to move mountains in Ohio. I started the ARC, encouraged the development of programs, I was a moving force in

200

getting a special camp up and running and kept it open when others wanted to close it. I sat on boards at local, county, and state levels. I went to national conferences as a representative for the rights of individuals with developmental disabilities. I was a behavior specialist and a therapist. Helping families every day, families who were in crisis. And now, here I was, unable to help my own daughter.

Toni's voice faded, "Okay, Linda, I will see what I can do."

"Thanks, Toni."

I waited to hear from someone Toni had talked with. Someone who could help. That call never came. The weekend before Christmas Irene and Sam left for their trip, leaving Jaime and Mark at home.

I invited Jaime and Mark to our home Christmas Eve and Christmas Day. The events and activities of the past few months left me feeling exhausted. I had to force myself to put up Christmas decorations, knowing it would be especially important for Jaime and Mark.

I told myself that maybe it would be better for Jaime and Mark with Irene and Sam gone. Maybe I could once again connect and help them over this rough time. Accepting disappointment about not being able to do something you want to do is a difficult step from the world of childhood into adulthood. A giant step toward maturity. By genetic disposition Jaime and Mark were destined to be childlike. It was highly likely they would never accept the subtleties and intricacies of maturity. How could I help them to understand about the inequities of life and create a buffer from unrealistic expectations?

Maturity and reality are nebulous things. Jaime has known for years that there is no Santa, but she continues to squeal with glee every time she sees one. It doesn't matter if they are tall and thin, short and round, if their beards are obviously fake, or if there is an entire group of Santas standing together. She has some special area of belief that blocks out reality and allows her to experience pure joy and the idea of being close to Santa Claus. She often breaks into a run and gives Santa a big hug before I can restrain or redirect her.

Jaime loves Santa and loves Christmas and I was determined to do everything in my power to make this a happy holiday.

Nothing Left

A phone rang. It seemed far away. It seemed to be part of a dream, but it wouldn't stop. I glanced at the clock – 3:00 A.M.. Who in the world could be calling? I fumbled around and found the receiver, "Hello?" I expected a wrong number or I would hear the blare of a fax call.

"Hello, Mrs. Tuttle – Linda Tuttle?"

It was a man and he was using my name. I woke up. "Yes, who is this?"

"I'm Officer Briggs. There's been a fire at Jaime's apartment. Could you come right now?"

"What? A fire?" The words burned in my mouth. "What...Jaime?" I had trouble forming words as the idea of a fire reached my mind and stomach at the same time. I barely whispered, "Is, is she okay?" My heart beat wildly, blood rushing to every part of my body. I was truly awake. "Oh, my God. Is she okay? Please..." The pleading cry surged forth before he had the chance to say anything.

"Yes ... yes, they're okay. I have them here with me. They're frightened, but okay. Could you come as soon as possible?"

"I'll be there in five minutes." I hung up the phone before I completed my sentence. I yelled at Ed who was still sound asleep, "Ed, there's been a fire. There's been a fire at Jaime's apartment." At the same time I grabbed at the clothes I'd taken off the previous evening.

From a sleepy haze Ed muttered, "What? A fire? What happened?"

"I don't know...I don't know. I just know the police called and said there was a fire. They want me to come as soon as possible."

"Hold on, I'll get dressed and come with you."

The urgency grew in my voice as I pulled on my shoes. "No, no time. I can't wait. I have to go. Right now."

"I can get ready quickly."

"No, no.... I have to go, now." My hands shook as I searched for my keys.

As I ran out the door Ed's voice trailed after me, "Be careful."

I hit the garage door opener as I ran to the car. The door lifted and the smell of smoke overpowered me. My stomach lurched. My God, they were three blocks away and I could smell the smoke. It was the middle of the night and there was no one out on the streets. I drove much faster than the 25 mph speed limit.

As I approached the parking lot I saw fire engines, police cars, and a group of people standing around, some in pajamas and robes, and others wrapped in blankets. Then I saw them. It was December 23rd and Jaime was standing there in the dark, wearing only a short sleeved nightshirt – no shoes and no robe. She was shaking. I will never know if it was from the cold or the shock of what just happened. Somehow I managed to park the car without running into anything or anyone. The minute I opened the car door I began to yell out, "Jaime. Jaime!"

She turned. She stood there looking at me with a blank stare. Almost as if she didn't recognize me.

"Jaime!"

She looked without smiling and flatly in a small voice said, "Mom."

I ran to her, leaving the car door open, "Jaime." I took her into my arms and hugged her. I then noticed Mark standing next to her, "Mark? Are you okay?"

He nodded. "I think Jaime's cold."

"Yes." I was trying to take in everything around us. It was too much, "Let's get both of you in the car. It'll be warmer there."

I walked them to the car and found a small, red plaid blanket in the trunk. I kept it in the car for times when I might stop at a park or the beach. Thank God it was here, Jaime was still shaking. I noticed Mark was fully dressed, "Okay, get into the car." When they settled into the front seat, I told Mark, "I need you to hug Jaime." I spread the blanket over them and covered as much as I could. "You two stay right here and don't move. Okay?"

They nodded in agreement.

I walked once again toward the crowd. I saw a woman I knew. "Jean? Do you know what happened?"

She shrugged, "All I know is there was a fire in their apartment. We've all been evacuated." She seemed less than friendly.

"Oh, my gosh, I'm so sorry."

She didn't respond.

I was feeling very much alone as I stood looking at the other people in the parking lot who had been ousted from their beds on this cold winter night. Just then, Ed arrived. I hadn't realized I was trembling until he put his arm around me. We didn't talk. The night was quiet. I could see ash floating in the air, it almost seemed like snowflakes.

A young policeman approached and asked, "Are you Linda Tuttle?"

I nodded.

He looked around, glanced at Jean and asked, "Do you know where they are?"

I spoke before she had the chance, "I put them in the car. Jaime was freezing. Can you tell me what happened?"

"Well, all I know is he started a fire. That's all I could get out of him. He seemed really confused. I don't know if they'll file charges against him or not."

"File charges? How bad is it?"

"Everything in their apartment is destroyed. The fire department is still putting out the fire."

I repeated a version of my earlier question, "How did it happen?"

"I don't know. We'll have to wait to find out. They have the investigator in there now."

"Can I go in?"

"No, they're still working. They don't know if it's in the walls and have to check the other apartments for possible damage."

"Oh, my God." The reality of the fire starting in their apartment frightened me all over again. I think the policeman thought I was going to start crying.

It was apparent he wasn't comfortable with raw emotions and took the opportunity to seek out more information, "I'll go find out." He walked away.

We stood there in the crowd of apartment dwellers who had been evicted from their warm beds in the middle of the night due to a fire started in Jaime and Mark's apartment. I was still trying to understand when a woman came up and said, "They never should have been allowed to live here."

"Excuse me?"

"They shouldn't be out on their own. We live next door to them and the fire alarm's always going off in the middle of the night. When it first happened I would walk around to the sliding glass doors to see if they were okay. Most of the time it was smoke from her trying to fix him French Toast – in the middle of the night! They never should have been allowed to live here."

"I'm sorry, I didn't know. No one told me." I would have cried, but I was empty, emptier than I had ever felt in my life. I looked around. All these people may lose their homes because of Jaime and Mark. It was too big, too much to hold. "I'm so sorry." What more could I say?

I turned to Ed who was holding me tightly, trying to stop my trembling. "I think we need to get the kids home. Would you take them? I can't leave."

"I want to stay here with you."

I nodded my head, "Yeah, I know, but Jaime needs to get into some warm clothes. Please?"

He agreed and as we walked toward the car the policeman seemed to appear out of thin air, "Mrs. Tuttle?"

"Yes?"

"If you're planning to leave, I want to verify a number for Mark. We're going to need to talk with him more."

"Why?"

"We think he started the fire on purpose."

"What? Mark? Started the fire – on purpose? I don't understand."

"We don't either right now."

"We need to take Jaime home to get some clothes on. She's freezing."

"Okay, just don't let them leave town."

My God, it was just like a movie, "Right." I nodded and shook my head at the same time.

Shortly after Ed left, the firemen gathered their equipment together. They told the residents they could return to their apartments to assess the damages. The first rays of dawn began to break through the darkness.

As I walked toward the apartment I could see a broken bedroom window. The firemen had used it to get rid of things in the apartment that were burned. Many of Jaime's and Mark's belongings were in a heap, just outside the window. I stopped, unable to move, as I looked at their possessions – now a large unidentifiable heap of smoldering smelly blackness lying next to the window. As I looked closely I saw strips of cloth with blackened edges that used to be clothing, discolored game boxes, a melted keyboard, bowling bags, and other charred clutter.

A fireman walked up, "This yours?"

"No. Yes. Well, sort of. My daughter and her husband lived here." It was obvious I wasn't functioning well.

"This stuff is still hot. Don't try to sift through it. Is there anything in particular you want?" He poked at pieces of clothing and I noticed a picture album.

"Can we see if there is anything left?" I pointed at the album. He used a long stick to drag it out and flipped it open. Pictures collapsed into the center of the book, like black lava flowing to the lowest point. A small piece of a picture that had not burned stood out. I could see Jaime, smiling, in her white wedding dress. Just then the next black page fell over it. He shoved it to the side, "Sorry, nothing to save."

Then he noticed something else, "Hey, is this a fireproof-box?"

"Oh, my gosh, it is – it's Jaime's box that she keeps all her personal papers in. Can we get it out?"

He struggled to remove it from the pile of smoldering embers. Wisps of steam rose from the box as it was exposed to the cool air. He commented, "You won't be able to touch it for a while."

I stood fixated on the charred blackened box while he poked through more of the black ruins. There was nothing else to save.

Ed returned and put his arm around me, "Are you okay?"

I couldn't speak. I nodded. He knew it was a lie and pulled me tightly to him. I felt trembling – was it him or me?

Ed asked the fireman, "Does anyone know what happened?"

"We know it started in the closet. The young man said something about going into the closet and dropping a candle. Has he had a history of starting fires?"

As the fireman's response hit me, I pushed away from Ed, "He started the fire? With a candle?"

The fireman nodded, "Looks that way. We just don't know if it was an accident or not. Does he have a history with fires?"

I shook my head, "Not that I know of. But, he loves fire engines. He often goes to the firehouse that's near his parents' home. He listens to the scanner to hear about the activities of the firemen."

I fell silent as I thought about this information and its possible meaning. I looked at the fireman and added, "He hasn't had any other trouble with starting fires, not since I've known him. But, I don't know a lot about his past."

I thought about his mother lying to me about him living on his own. About her withholding his history of raging behaviors. What else had she not told me?

Ed's voice broke into my thoughts, "Can we go in?"

The fireman nodded, "Yes. I think its okay now. We have all our equipment out. I'll warn you, there's not much left. What the fire didn't destroy, the water did."

His warning was not sufficient to prepare us. As I stepped in, I wasn't ready for the intensity of the smoke. It hung in the air, entering my nose and my mouth. I took a breath and coughed as it entered my lungs. I wanted to run, but I was transfixed. Everything was covered in a layer of black. Water dripped from the ceilings and walls. As I walked into the bedroom, I felt the water entering my shoes. Black. Everything was black, burnt, charred. Gone. Everything was gone.

The fireman broke the silence, "I have to go."

We nodded simultaneously.

"Don't forget your daughter's fireproof-box." You might be needing some of the papers in there."

We nodded again and watched him leave. He seemed very tall in his full attire of high black boots, black pants, black coat with a yellow stripe, and his fireman's hat. He almost seemed to be an apparition as he faded into the morning light.

Ed's arm around me seemed to be the only thing holding me up, "Honey, we need to get back to the kids."

I nodded, but didn't move. I couldn't leave. "I have to stay. There's no way to secure anything."

He looked around and giving a hollow laugh he said, "What are you worried about securing?"

I didn't know, but I couldn't leave. "You go back, check on the kids. We have to call Sam and Irene...Oh, no!" My legs gave out and I dropped onto a nearby blackened wooden chair.

"What? What now?"

"We don't have a phone number to reach them. Irene said she didn't want to hear from Mark."

"Son of bitch! I can't believe it."

"Huh." Followed by a flat, empty laugh, "me either." I looked around. "Uh...she probably gave the information to his sister or David. Have Mark give you their numbers and tell them what happened. I'll come home in a little while. I just can't leave right now. I have to think through everything."

Thoughts of the past few months crowded my mind. All the warning signs that things weren't going well. The chronic issues with Irene, before the wedding and after. Was there anything I could have done, should have done, that would have stopped this from happening? I needed to be alone with my thoughts and try to make some sense out the entire situation – if that would be possible.

Ed didn't like leaving me. But he understood I couldn't leave – wouldn't leave. He handed me a cell phone, "Please call if you need me." He kissed me lightly, sensing that I might break apart if he wasn't careful.

Cleaning Up

I wandered through the apartment again. Opening closet and cupboard doors, everything was covered with black soot. The towels in the bathroom closet took on a tarnished look with burnished brown edges created from the heat. Everything plastic morphed from the original shape to a melted blob. Nails holding plasterboards in place popped out of their seams, giving the walls and ceilings a strange and eerie look. My gaze fell on the Christmas tree. It seemed so out of place. All the Christmas gifts had been in the closet. All were gone.

The candle holder from the wedding ceremony sat on the coffee table. There was one candle missing. The one in the middle. The candle that represented Mark's and Jaime's union. It must have been the candle Mark used to start the fire. My heart lurched and my hand covered my mouth to hold in the scream that had been waiting for release since the policeman called about the fire.

It was six o'clock in the morning, still too early to call anyone – anyone except my mother who lived in Florida. Sometimes there was an advantage to the three hour time difference. Hopefully, she would be home. I needed to talk with someone. I reached for the phone and started to dial. No dial tone. Of course, everything electrical or with circuits, was melted. Thank goodness Ed brought my cell phone. My fingers shook as I pushed the numbers. As much as I wanted to talk to my mother, I was afraid. Afraid to share with anyone the thoughts I was having about this entire horrible happening.

She answered on the first ring, "Hello."

"Mom?"

"What's wrong?" She immediately knew the tone of my voice was pleading for a mother's comfort.

For the first time I started to cry and between sobs I said, "Oh, Mom, it's horrible. Everything is burnt."

"Where? What are you talking about?"

"Jaime's apartment. Mark started a fire. Everything is gone."

"Is Jaime okay?"

"Yes. Thank God they're both okay." The miles dissolved and I felt calmer hearing my mother remind me that material possessions can be replaced. The most important thing was no one was physically injured. As I hung up I knew we would be okay.

Over the next couple of hours I made a number of such calls. To Jaime's brother, Jaime's work, Mary the social worker, and Toni. Toni said she was on her way. She was coming to help clean up.

I had just set the cell phone down when Ed called, "What do I do with Jaime?"

"Huh? What do you mean?"

"Linda, she has no clothes. The only thing she has is that short nightshirt she's wearing."

"Oh! I'll come home and find something of mine she can wear. We'll have to go shopping later. Toni's going to be here in about an hour. I'll be right there."

I locked the door as I was leaving and walking to the parking lot I passed the pile of unidentifiable burnt belongings which were next to the window. I laughed. The idea of locking a door when there was a large, open, gaping hole where the window had been gave an indication of how bizarre everything was – how disoriented I felt.

When I arrived at the house Ed met me outside. "Linda, I'm really worried about Mark. He's just sitting there and rocking in the chair. He doesn't respond to questions. What should we do?"

I shrugged my shoulders. I was beyond answers. I hugged him and went into the house.

Jaime and Mark heard me coming. Mark moved from the chair to the couch, next to Jaime. They sat there, not talking, just sitting, as if they were waiting for the arrival of a train or bus that could whisk them away to some place where they would not have to face the reality of the past few hours.

Mark was the first to speak, "Can we go home now?"

I didn't know how to answer him. I shook my head. "There's no place to go back to. The apartment is ruined."

Jaime started to cry. Mark held her, but didn't seem to grasp the reality of the situation. He told Jaime, "It's okay. My mom will fix it."

I walked away. It was the safest thing I could do.

The rest of the day was a blur. Toni brought two other friends, Carole and Sandy, to help sort through things and move Jaime's belongings back home, anything that appeared remotely salvageable. Thank goodness there was still running water. Everything had to be washed several times. I bought a case of paper towels and bottles of cleaning fluids, disinfectants, and fabric fresheners. Before wrapping anything to go into storage, every item was washed and given a liberal dose of fabric freshener, in hopes that the smoky odor would dissipate.

When I saw Toni going through the kitchen cupboards, I told her to leave everything. Most of it had been gifts from Mark's side of the family and I did not want to be accused of taking something that belonged to them. The only salvageable thing from the bedroom was a dresser of Jaime's made of Formica. The only thing wrong was some heat damage to one side. It gave me a new appreciation for Formica. All of the clothing in the drawers had tinges of black or brown. Amazing. It was like food rotting from the inside, but the outside looked okay. We took some of the paintings from the living room walls, a few glass and metal items, and cans of food. The majority of Jaime's belongings were thrown away.

I assigned Jaime and Mark the job of taking the ornaments off the tree, washing and wrapping those that could be saved. Intermittently Mark would laugh. When asked what was funny, he couldn't or wouldn't answer.

By early afternoon we were back at our home. A few boxes were stacked on one side of the garage. Even after washing everything several times before packing them, everything reeked from the stench of smoke. I knew within a few days most of those items would be thrown away. Every time someone opened the door to the garage the odor of smoke would invade our home.

Mark's parents arrived in the late afternoon. Seeing them brought a renewed sense of overwhelm and disbelief. It was the first time I felt a real rapport with them. I could see my own feelings in the stress and worry expressed in their eyes and facial expressions. They were relieved to see both Mark and Jaime had not been hurt physically, but they were confused. What happened? How did it happen? I told them what I knew and explained there were no clear answers.

I talked with Sam privately, giving him all the information I had been given by the firemen and police. "Sam, I'm worried about Mark. I think he's had a total mental breakdown."

I wanted to tell him from a professional perspective that Mark should be committed to a locked facility. But I wasn't sure it was a professional opinion. Most likely it would have been Jaime's mother speaking. I couldn't separate my two disparate parts. The mother had taken over. I was too close and too tired to be professional.

Sam was tentative but seeking help, "What do you think we should do?"

"I don't know. I'm sorry, but I really don't know. What I do know is Mark can't stay here. He'll have to go home with you. I'm worried about your safety. The only advice I have is to watch him closely."

Sam nodded his head. He had nothing to say. I had nothing to say. All sound and fury had been sucked out of the day. Sam and Irene motioned to Mark and they left. Ed, Jaime, and I stood watching at the door. We didn't wave or move until their car disappeared from the street. I pulled Jaime to me. The smell of smoke still hung in her freshly washed hair. My heart hurt as the odor set off a flood of fear and pain from the last few hours and confusion about where to go and what to do next.

I hugged her before saying, "Okay, I think we need to get you some clothes. Let's go."

Kindness

Shopping was the last thing I wanted to do, but I forced myself. There was no choice. Jaime had no clothing, not even a pair of underpants, a bra, or socks. Entering the store and hearing Christmas carols caused waves of feelings: anger, frustration, confusion, sadness, emptiness, and then happiness and joy. I was angry and frustrated at the situation and at Mark's mother. I felt empty and confused when I thought about the future. Happy that Jaime was not living with Mark and that she was safe. Sad that her dreams had just gone up in smoke.

When there is any type of tragedy or trauma, there's a natural tendency to talk about it – over and over again. Somehow it seems if we talk about it enough, we can make sense of the injustices and set things into perspective. We can release the internal, pent-up pressure through verbal venting. I couldn't seem to stop myself from telling the clerks what happened to Jaime and why we needed to find clothing.

Finding clothing for most people is not a major task, but finding clothing that fits Jaime's short square body is more than a little difficult. Store clerks went out of their way to seek items that might fit and to explore the possibility of additional discounts. One clerk said, "I'll bet you don't have any hangers."

I laughed at her insight and logical conclusion and my inability to wrap my mind around all the details that would need to be considered within the next few days. "Hangers – yes, we need them.   We need everything." I started to cry.

Jaime reached up and patted my arm, "I okay, Mom. It okay. No cry."

I wiped away the tears, smiled at Jaime and the clerk, "Yes, we need hangers and yes, we will be okay."

The clerk loaded us up with a huge bag of hangers – no charge – good things do happen. We found clerks everywhere kind, helpful, and resourceful, thinking of things I didn't.

The next day I kept receiving concerned calls from people who had heard about what happened. One such call came from the director of Jaime's work program. "Linda, I'm so sorry to hear about what happened.   Several people have asked if they can donate money, clothing, or furniture to help Jaime."

It was so unexpected and so kind. Over the years I had done much to help other people.   This was the first time I felt in desperate need, but at the same time I wasn't sure what I needed.   I was nodding, but hadn't said anything, and finally found my voice. "That would be so nice. I don't know what to even tell you she needs. She needs clothing – everything, she needs everything. Everything was destroyed."

"I know, Toni told us about how extensive the damage was, that's why we would like to help."

"Yes, Toni, Carole, and Sandy came over to try to save stuff, but there really wasn't much worth saving."

"Well, if it's okay, we'll take donations and set up a fund for Jaime."

What could I say? We had spent a significant amount in the short time we were out, just to get a few basics. "Yes....and thank you."

The next unexpected call came from a member of our church. The church group had also started a fund for Jaime. Everyone's kindness was overwhelming.

Christmas

December 24th has always been a special time when we call family who live back east, drive around to admire Christmas lights, and return home to tasty treats of shrimp and crab served with crispy crackers and eggnog. For years Mark had been with us on Christmas Eve. Early Christmas Eve day Jaime asked if he could come over. I hesitated, but not for long. "No, not tonight, honey. We're all too tired. I haven't slept in two days and I don't think you have either."

Jaime's eyes filled with tears. It seemed every time I looked at her since the fire her eyes were glassy. I wondered if it would be a permanent condition. I reached out to hug her. I could not touch her enough. It was as if I had to verify she was real and safe. "I'm sorry. I can't have Mark come over tonight. We'll be going to bed early. I called the doctor to get medication that will help you sleep."

Jaime nodded and without saying another word, she went to her room. I assumed she was calling Mark to tell him he was not invited.

Within minutes the phone rang. It was Mark's mother. She wanted to know if they could come by Christmas Day and if Mark could visit with Jaime. I agreed. Irene said they would be here at noon.

I was so exhausted. I told Jaime I just could not do our traditional Christmas Eve. We didn't go out. I didn't fix any special food or drink. We watched some Christmas program on TV and I suggested we go to bed early in hopes that we might sleep.

I gave Jaime the sedative prescribed by the doctor, but it wasn't too effective. Within an hour after going to bed I heard Jaime crying. I went to her and held her until she drifted off. This happened several times.

Throughout the night I kept waking up to a phone ringing. I picked it up, but there was only dial tone. It took awhile until I realized the phone was part of my dreams. Each time I would set the receiver back in its cradle and pray myself back to sleep. Morning came much too early. Another night with constantly interrupted sleep. I wondered if we would ever sleep soundly again.

I fixed our traditional breakfast of cinnamon rolls, shaped into a Christmas tree and decorated with green and white frosting. Normally they were devoured quickly amid Christmas bantering as presents were checked out and shaken, everyone trying to make last minute guesses before opening them. This year we ate in silence. Somehow the cinnamon rolls tasted like cardboard. Opening gifts seemed unimportant, but we did it instinctively. Although we had much to be thankful for, the Christmas glow was tarnished. Habits and traditions pulled us through and gave us direction.

Midmorning the phone rang and Ed answered it. He then waved for me to come to him. He was giving monosyllabic responses, "Yeah...no....uh huh...okay... oh. I think you should talk with Linda first." He covered the receiver as he said, "It's Carl, Jaime's Dad. I didn't just want to let him talk with Jaime until you talked to him."

It was the first time I had talked with Carl since his letter. I didn't want to talk to him. I knew Jaime would. I took the phone as if I was holding a snake. I didn't want to put the receiver next to my ear, but I did, "Yes?"

"Merry Christmas, Linda."

"Hm," was all I managed to say. "What do you want?"

"I want to talk with Jaime. I heard what happened. Is she okay?"

"As well as can be expected. She doesn't need anymore disappointments and she sure as hell doesn't need anyone lecturing her – especially you."

"That's not what I called for. I wanted to talk with her, to tell her I'm sorry. To let her know I love her."

"That's a revelation."

"Could you save it? I'm concerned about Jaime."

"Really? I never would have known."

"Seriously, Linda, I want to help her. Can we do anything?"

"She needs a lot right now. But most of all she needs people to love her and accept her for who she is – no questions, no judgments, and certainly none of your crappy shit."

"Okay, I get it. I said I'm sorry. Can I talk with her?"

I knew how much it would mean for Jaime to hear from her dad. "Okay."

Jaime was elated. It was like Santa Claus paying her a special visit. I resented that he could be forgiven so easily. But I was happy to see her smile. Their phone call went well, and as usual, Jaime held no grudges.

When Mark arrived with his parents, each entered carrying boxes of gifts. I felt detached from everything that was happening. As I watched, I thought absurdly about the three wise men who visited Jesus. I certainly didn't feel there was anything wise about these three. I should have been appreciative, but instead I just felt weird.

Sitting and watching Jaime open gifts from Mark and his parents, I became aware of an anger which had woven itself around my heart and was making it difficult for me to breathe. I wanted them all to leave. I wanted them out of my home and out of Jaime's life. I wanted to rewind time and to stop Jaime and Mark from ever marrying. That was the only thing that could make this right and that wasn't about to happen.

After Jaime opened all the gifts, Sam went outside with Mark. They came back in carrying a television. Irene announced it was only fair that Mark replace

Jaime's TV. Mark's mood seemed to darken. I guessed his TV had not been replaced. It was obvious this gift was difficult for Mark to part with. Sam and Irene seemed oblivious to Mark's change of mood. How bizarre. I wondered how often throughout Mark's life his thoughts and feelings had been ignored. It was sad. Everything seemed sad. The anger I felt was replaced by a deep sense of sorrow. Maybe not replaced, but interlaced in a complex pattern of dark colors making it impossible to see which was which.

Jaime seemed to sense Mark's unhappiness over the TV and immediately tuned her attention to her other presents. Irene gave Jaime several skirts and blouses. Jaime held each one up for everyone to admire and then she decided to do a fashion show. Seeing Jaime performing, twirling around, smiling, and bowing lightened the mood. It was amazing – everything Irene purchased fit.

The day went well. Irene and Sam only stayed a short time. It was difficult for all of us. We were being hospitable, but there was an undeniable tension. Everyone was uncomfortable. Jaime and Mark were the only ones who seemed unabashed by the entire event. They were happy to be together. It was like nothing ever happened. But it had.

Later that evening I called Irene to thank her. She said, "Well, I know Jaime is a clothes horse and we wanted to help replace some of what was lost. By the way, I want to talk about what we need to do to get the kids back together."

I shouldn't have been surprised at the suggestion, but I was, "I don't know what to tell you. Right now I am not ready to suggest they get back together. It's too soon."

"Well, you know they are married."

"I know that."

"So they should be together."

"I am not ready to talk about this. We'll talk later." And I did what she had done so many times to me. I hung up the phone without giving her the opportunity to say anything else. Truth was I didn't know what to say because I had been much too busy taking care of the aftermath of the fire to sort out my thoughts and feelings.

When I sat down that evening to relax, for what seemed like the first time since the fire, I turned on the TV to watch the local news. My heart sank and stomach lurched as I listened to the newscaster describing a fire that happened Christmas Eve. Two children were burned to death just a few blocks from our home. The pictures of the burned apartment building connected with my internal pain. The black streaks reached upward from the gaping holes where windows used to be. I was flooded with the odor of smoke. A sensation of heat ran through my body and then cold. My God, I was so cold. I pulled a nearby comforter over me, but I could not get warm. I heard Jaime crying and ran to her. She had been watching the news about the fire and dead children and was shaking uncontrollably. "Why, Mom, why?"

I had no good answer. I held her tightly. "I don't know Jaime. I don't know." I had said that a million times to myself since the fire happened – Why? I don't know. In an effort to reach for a comforting thought I told her, "Jaime, Mark was just not able to handle being married. It was too much for him. Too much for you. It was just too much." My voice trailed off. It was all too much.

Ed and I talked many times about the series of events that led up to the wedding and subsequently to the fire. I found myself repeating myself, over and over, about how I should have known. How I should have seen what was happening and how I should have intervened earlier.

Ed reminded me that I had been supportive and tried on numerous occasions to offer help. It was always met with resistance and when I thought Jaime might be in danger I tried to talk her into coming home. He reminded me, as Jaime often told me, "She is an adult." Jaime's favorite phrase, used to shut me down each time I tried to discuss her problems with Mark, was "I am adult." End of subject. Could I have pushed her more? Been more insistent? I worried that if I tried, she would withdraw more and shut me out completely. As I went over and over and over the events of Jaime's and Mark's life together, I honestly did not think I could have done anything differently.

In some ways the fire was an answer to a prayer. Jaime was home and safe. I couldn't think of anything else that would have made her return. She was safe. I said that after each thought of the fire and gave thanks for her safety

Now we had to deal with the emotional destruction and repercussions. I knew Irene and Sam were going through the same torments, but I couldn't find any place within me to feel sad for them. I felt sad for

Jaime and sad for Mark, but toward Irene and Sam I could only feel anger. Anger over lies and omissions filled the space where empathy might have grown.

Life Goes On

The day after Christmas Jaime asked to go back to work. I was worried it was too soon, but she insisted and I didn't want to be another obstacle for her to overcome, so I allowed her to return. I returned to my work at the clinic. My work involved therapy and assessment for children and their families. Intrusive thoughts of Jaime and Mark disrupted my ability to think clearly. Returning to work was not easy; I couldn't concentrate.

Irene called me at the clinic several times. She never seemed to understand I could not entertain personal issues in the midst of tending to my clients' trauma. Finally, I set a boundary with her. I told her not to call me at work. If she had something to say, it would have to wait until evening.

The phone rang as I entered the house that same night, "Hello."

It was Irene, "Hello. Can you talk now?" There was a definite edge to her question. She was obviously not happy at having to wait and wanted me to know it.

"I just this moment walked in the door."

"Well, exactly when can you take the time to talk about your daughter?"

I set my purse down and fell into a nearby chair. Now my voice carried an edge, "Alright, Irene. What do you want?"

"We have to talk about what is going to happen with Jaime and Mark."

"Okay." I decided to be as brief as possible. "And?"

"What does that mean?"

"Listen, Irene, I'm tired. I'm really not in the mood to talk, but you insisted. What do you want?"

"Well," she paused before continuing "I think they need to get back together as soon as possible and I've been talking to their caseworker. Mary said she might be able to find a place, a group home where they could live together."

"What?" Having worked in the system I knew if a group home accepted Mark, they would be housing other men who had been in trouble. Fire setting was a behavior that demanded a high level of care. Usually these homes housed dangerous clients known for physical or sexual aggression. Could I have heard her correctly? She wanted Jaime to move to one of these homes with Mark? My immediate thoughts were, *No way in hell.* I hated thinking of fires and fiery places so the next thought suited me better, *When hell freezes over.* But, I didn't say either of those. Instead I heard myself say, "I want to talk with Mary."

"Good, she wants to talk with you so she can make the arrangements."

Irene heard what she wanted to hear and I was in no mood to dissuade her. "Okay, Irene. I'll talk with her." Then I decided to let her know I wasn't inclined to follow her suggestion. "I'll talk. That doesn't mean I'll agree." With that I hung up the phone. I was beginning to gain some satisfaction from being the first one to hang up.

The next day I called the caseworker, Mary. I had no idea what to expect. Was she going to threaten me if I didn't agree to allow Jaime to go with Mark? After all, the previous case worker threatened me when Jaime wanted to marry Jeremy. Now I wished we hadn't won the battle with Jeremy. I couldn't go there. We can never change the past. I had to deal with what was happening right now.

Before calling Mary I decided to phone an attorney. I wanted to know if I had any rights. Mr. Davis, the attorney, was wonderful. He did a lot of work with individuals with developmental disabilities. He had already heard about the fire.

He did not waste time, but immediately asked, "Does Jaime want a divorce?"

I shook my head, "I don't think so. She insists she still loves him."

"Well, have you thought about having their marriage annulled?"

"No. I didn't think it would be possible."

He hesitated only a moment, "Maybe not. We would need to talk more, but I think it might be possible."

He indicated he wasn't sure, but certainly the fire would have an impact on how the court would look at their ability to live independently. Information about Mark had been withheld; their marriage was founded on lies. He then went on to explain I might be able to have Jaime conserved, which would mean she couldn't be married. I learned a lot from the short conversation with the attorney.

Information was power. The attorney, Mr. Davis, offered options. He also assured us he would support us in not allowing Jaime to be moved to a group home filled with male deviants.

When I called Mary, I was ready. Immediately I told her I had contacted an attorney and would not approve of Jaime and Mark living together in some group home meant for men with behavioral problems. Mary let me know she had not recommended it. She explained she only agreed to look into it. She said it was unlikely they would even be able to find such a place. She understood my position and would support that decision.

I called Irene and told her that I could not, under any circumstance, approve of Jaime moving to a group home with Mark. In fact, I could not approve of her moving back with Mark. Initially, she responded with silence. Then told me she was shocked and dismayed that I would stand between a husband and wife. Her words were like bullets, aimed to hurt. I didn't care. I had the caseworker and an attorney on my side. I was ready for battle.

When most of the venom was released, Irene asked, "Are you planning to keep Jaime from seeing Mark?"

"No, that's not my intention. I just won't agreed to them living together." I didn't tell her about the visit to the attorney. I did suggest we take things slowly. I shared Jaime was still not able to sleep at night, even with the sedative the doctor had given her. I told Irene Jaime would be seeing a therapist. I was worried she may be suffering from Posttraumatic Stress Disorder.

My next phone call was to Nancy, a therapist I worked with and admired. When I told her what had happened, she immediately made an appointment to see us.

Decisions

In addition to daily phone calls, Jaime and Mark continued to see each other on weekends. The arrangement seemed agreeable to everyone, except Irene. Jaime began sleeping through the night and after several weeks Mark appeared more like himself. At times Jaime would smile and laugh. I felt like I could breathe without inhaling the odor of smoke. Sometimes I wondered about the apartment and if the police had ever been to talk with Mark, but I decided not to ask. I purposefully stayed away from going near the apartment and avoided talking with Irene and Sam. Life was beginning to feel normal again.

It was February and Mark was visiting Jaime. They were in her bedroom when I heard his voice raise with a menacing tone. I found myself running toward her room before my thoughts registered. It was instinctual. I opened the door without knocking. Jaime was sitting on the bed and he was standing over her, with his fist in the air. I yelled, "Mark! Stop it!"

He turned and glared at me. "This is between me and my wife."

"Not in my house. You will not yell at Jaime, nor will you ever hit her. Ever."

He stared at me. His frozen glare told me he was debating about what to do or say next.

I spoke first, "Mark, I think you better get ready. I'm taking you home."

"I'm not done talking to Jaime."

"Yes, you are. Get ready right this minute."

"But…"

"There are no buts. You are frightening Jaime and I will not allow it."

"I want to go to a parade."

"What?"

"I want to go to the drummer's parade. My uncle is going to take us. Jaime said she won't go and she has to go. She's my wife and has to do what I say."

Jaime was now crying.

"Mark, it is obvious Jaime doesn't want to go. I don't think you two should be seeing each other." It was out of my mouth before I knew I was saying it. Jaime did not object.

"My mother won't let that happen."

"Your mother has nothing to do with this."

"We'll see about that."

"Yes, we will."

I told Jaime to stay at the house while I took Mark home. We rode in silence and separated without a word when he got out of the car.

That night the phone rang. It was Irene and she launched directly into her speech which I could tell was practiced, "Mark said you will not allow Jaime to go to the parade with him. You know that David will be taking them and he'll watch them. So, there is no reason for them not to go. Mark also said you wouldn't allow him to talk about it with Jaime. Linda, they need to have private time and work through what happened to them. Mark said you told him he wasn't going to see Jaime anymore and I wanted to let you know it is not your decision." She said all of that without a breath.

"Are you done?"

"What?"

"I wanted to know if you said everything you called to say."

She paused, this was a different Linda she was talking with and she wasn't sure what to say or do next.

I continued, "Irene, you weren't here. Mark was being mean to Jaime. She doesn't like noisy drums and parades because the sound bothers her. Mark wouldn't listen. He yelled at her and when I entered the room it looked as if he might be getting ready to hit her. I won't have it. I'm taking Jaime to see an attorney – tomorrow."

"What? What for?"

"I'm going to find out if Jaime can get an annulment, or if that isn't possible, a divorce. There is absolutely nothing you or Mark can say or do about this. Jaime has not been able to protect herself, so I am going to take charge."

"But..."

I cut her off, "There are no buts. This is it. The end." I hung up the phone.

I discussed the idea with Ed and Jaime of following through with the annulment. I knew I would never allow her to go back to living alone with Mark again. I thought about him moving in with us; but I did not trust his ability to be separated from his mother without becoming overwhelmed and therefore dangerous. I was hoping it might work for Jaime and Mark to just be able to see each other. To return to a situation where they were dating, but that was no longer an option. We were out of options. They could no longer be together – ever.

Mark threatening Jaime caused her to relapse. She was unresponsive for the rest of the day after Mark's outrage. I would never allow him to threaten her again. It was clear they could no longer be together.

The next day we went to see the attorney. Jaime went with us. It was difficult and she kept saying, "But, I love him." I held her and tried to comfort her, but there was nothing or no one who could stop me from proceeding with legal action to end the marriage that was fashioned from fantasy and love, but built on ignorance and lies.

Finding Hope

Our next stop was at the therapist's office. Nancy developed a beautiful rapport with Jaime. Within minutes she gently encouraged Jaime to review what had happened and helped her to link past experiences with what took place over the weekend. She posed questions to assist Jaime with separating a desire for a loving relationship from the reality of her fear-provoking relationship with Mark.

Walking into Nancy's office was interesting and fun. Two walls were filled with shelves holding a multitude of miniature items and figurines. One of the interventions Nancy was famous for was Sand Tray work. The client is invited to place objects and figurines of their choosing into a two by three foot wooden tray which is filled with several inches of sand. The concept invites someone to nonverbally express themselves through the use of symbolic objects. I had worked with a sand tray at graduate school and had used it several times with my clients. Neither of those practices prepared me for the work Jaime and I were about to engage in.

Nancy gave us each a sand tray and asked for us to use the miniatures on the walls and create our own design which would represent our experience of what happened. She encouraged us to walk around and look at all the little toys, to pick them up and, when attracted to one, to set it to the side. Soon we each had a pile of miniatures next to our trays. We worked independently on our individual sand trays, placing an object or figure in the sand, evaluating it, and rearranging it until everything felt right.

Jaime's sand tray replicated the apartment with fire trucks and police cars surrounding it. Nancy then asked her to talk about her sand tray. Jaime shared the story of the night of the fire and moved the figurines around as she talked.

We learned some additional terrifying information as Jaime moved through the events of that night. While the female figure was sleeping on the couch, the male figurine, representing Mark, took a lit candle from the candelabra and went to the closet. He threw the candle into the closet and watched while it began to burn. She then walked the figurine back to the living room. He yelled at Jaime to wake up. She used a deep voice and said, "Fire, Jaime. A fire. I call fire department."

She moved her figurine into the bedroom and went to the closet to get a coat. She reenacted opening the closet door. The figurine jumped back and she blew on her hand. Of course – the door knob had been hot. She then picked up Mark's figurine and moved it right behind her figurine. We aren't sure what may have happened. She dropped the figurines and totally collapsed. She couldn't stop crying. She refused to answer any of our questions. Could he have tried to push her into the closet? It was the only thing that made sense, but she refused to talk about it.

I held her until she stopped crying, until her shoulders stopped quivering, and her chest stopped heaving. Over and over again I whispered, "It is okay. You're safe now."

She looked up at me with a tear streaked face and reddened eyes, "Why?"

I took a breath and hugged her, "I don't know. But you are safe now."

"I love him."

My heart skipped a beat, "I know."

"I don't trust him." She once again dissolved into tears. It was the first time she had admitted anything other than "I love him."

We left shortly after that. Nancy took pictures of our sand trays and we agreed to reconstruct mine on the next visit. She asked me to write a story about it, "You know like 'Once upon a time.'" I worked on it until we saw her again.

My sand tray items were chosen for their symbolism. The first piece was an unidentifiable clay figurine inside a cave. Behind that figurine was an angel and right behind her was a candle holder with three candles. I took one candle out. Off to the side I placed a painted green egg with a very sad face. In front of that I put a small heart. Next to the green egg I placed a ghostly figure. In front of the figurine in the cave I placed a lady who had the body of a butterfly. Her hands were stretched outward and held the ends of her wings. Directly in front of that I placed a full butterfly with an angel next to it.

Following is my story:

"Once upon a time a beautiful princess was born. Her parents loved her dearly. She was different from other children. She was kinder and sweeter than most. Everyone who knew her loved her.

When she grew up she met a prince who fell in love with her. They got married. At first everything seemed wonderful, but the prince wanted to keep the princess all to himself. He made her work all the time and he began to yell at the princess and treated her cruelly. The princess' mother wanted to help, but the prince kept the princess in a cave and couldn't let anyone near her, especially not the mother. (I pointed at the figures as I told the story. Jaime was the figurine in the cave.) The mother became frightened, so scared she felt sick. (I pointed to the sad faced green egg.) She loved the princess so much and worried terribly.

She sent out love to the princess and she prayed. (My finger touched the heart by the green egg.) She didn't think God was listening to her prayers. She felt the Holy Spirit (the ghostly figurine) must be watching, but no one seemed to be able to get to the princess to save her.

The prince got sicker and sicker until one night he started a fire. The mother's prayers were answered. An angel (the angel in front of the candles) was there and she protected the princess. The prince could no longer keep the princess captive and when the princess escaped she became like a beautiful butterfly who had been held in a cocoon (the half woman /half butterfly figure). She was free again to spread her wings and fly with other beautiful butterflies. The mother was happy because she now knew without a doubt that the angels would always watch over the princess and protect her."

When I finished reading my story, Jaime grabbed me so hard she almost pulled me over. Once again she was whole-heartedly sobbing and she continued to cry for more than fifteen minutes. It could have been a half hour. Something happened with my sharing of the fairy tale. We all knew it touched her deeply; a change had taken place. She then started to laugh and cry at the same time. We just held each other. Both of us crying and intermittently laughing. I wasn't sure why I was laughing, except Jaime's laugh was infectious – as were her tears. I began to feel lighter and better than I had since the entire event started. Jaime wiped her face with a tissue and handed one to me.

She said, "I okay, Mom. I okay."

This time I believed her. She was okay. We were okay. The worst was behind us.

We continued to see Nancy for several months. She helped us through the rough spots of obtaining an annulment. One day when we went for our regularly scheduled therapy appointment Jaime surprised me. She announced to Nancy, "I done."

Nancy looked at me and I shrugged my shoulders, letting her know I had had no advance warning of Jaime's pronouncement.

Nancy continued with Jaime, "What do you mean?"

Jaime broke into a big smile, "I done! I be happy." She said it with such a sense of assurance and completion that Nancy and I both understood she meant she was finished with therapy.

We were astonished. Nancy suggested we have at least one closure meeting. Jaime was pleased with that. "I bring music. I show you."

I knew Jaime had been listening to a lot of music in her room and had appeared happier during the past week. But, I hadn't expected her to end therapy. I thought it would take years.

The Final Song

When it was time to go to therapy, Jaime carried her CD player with her. She would not discuss it with me, saying "Wait. I show you and Nancy."

Immediately after entering Nancy's office, Jaime methodically set everything up before she would say a word. She positioned the CD player directly in front of

Nancy and me. Before she started playing any music, Jaime showed us the cover of Barbara Streisand's CD *A Love Like Ours* and bowed. She was intent on making this a presentation, and it was clear she was in charge. She then began to move back and forth through the songs, sometimes only using a line or a part of a line from a song.

She started with a song titled, 'I've Dreamed of You.' Barbara Streisand's soft melodious tones shared a story of searching and praying for love and almost giving in to thoughts of never finding love when she meets the love of her life. Sadness and fear fade when they make a commitment and marry. Only feelings of happiness remain for a couple blessed with love and friendship.

She was very selective of the lyrics she wanted us to hear. It took great effort to stop the song at just the right place and move to the next. So, she devised a method of using the sign language and signed "stop" and "go" so we would know what part she wanted us to listen to.

Jaime moved to one song after another expressing the deep emotions and joy of new love.

She then turned and looked at us and said, "Listen." From the song, 'If You Ever Leave Me' she chose words that expressed concern that love may not be forever and yet there is a desire to continue and not return to loneliness.

Jaime became intense as she struggled to find the right song lyric, then relaxed when she played a few lines from, 'It Must Be You.' I felt a chill go through me as I listened to the words which shared how a woman changes for a man. Recognizing the changes, she feels helpless. She will do and say things out of character.

She moved to the next song, 'We Must Be Loving Right' and started it with a part explaining how some people seem to have more trouble and do not have much happiness. Friends begin to notice there is trouble and talk about love fading.

Now Jaime was focused on the machine and was too involved to acknowledge anyone else was in the room. Her next selection, 'If I Never Met You" showed a wisdom that seemed beyond her age or comprehension. The song spoke of appreciation for having the opportunity to know love and without it her life would have been even sadder and filled with regret.

She then went back to, 'If You Ever Leave Me' for just a few words about anger and lies and a flame that burned in the darkness.

I looked at Nancy and she at me. Our faces said it all, we were both stunned. The next piece was equally unsettling. 'If I Didn't Love You' started with the idea of being safe from harm and never feeling the pain. It shared a wish for peace and for their love to be saved. The haunting voice suggested if only he would say he was sorry, maybe it wouldn't need to end.

She again stopped the music. The words she had chosen were powerful and we sensed her pain. I reached for a Kleenex.

We thought she was finished until she pulled another CD out of her backpack. Again, it was Barbara Streisand's. This time it was *Higher Ground*.

She looked at me before pushing the start button and said, "This Mom."

Jaime moved directly to a song, 'If I Could.' This song spoke to a desire to protect someone, and yet understanding there is a higher power at work within all situations, even when we don't see it and we begin to lose faith. It questions the heartaches and ends with the reassurance that there are reasons for everything and lessons to learn.

It continued in a haunting manner that only Barbara Streisand can make happen. The song encouraged one not to give up and to let our heart guide us. If we keep on believing we will find the answer to the most profound lesson of all – we can learn how to love ourselves.

Jaime turned off the CD player, the room filled with silence. Jaime looked at us. When there was no immediate reaction she held her hands up and said, "See?"

Nancy and I sat in awe. Neither of us could speak. There were no words to express our current feelings and the wonder for what Jaime had just shared and admiration for how she did it.

Nancy looked at me, "Did you know? Did you help her with this?"

I shook my head.

Jaime's brow furrowed, she didn't understand why we had not immediately responded. Her voice raised, "See? I done. I be happy – now."

One more time I found myself crying, but this time it was tears of joy. Jaime had managed to work through the fear and trauma of what happened to her.

The pain from the loss she had experienced. And possibly the most amazing shift was from the heart-rending disappointment of the relationship she hoped would last a lifetime, but it didn't. It had ended. Her music selection demonstrated an understanding of everything that had happened to her. She even found phrases relating to fire and burning that accented the meaning for her sharing.

What I found most amazing was after everything that had happened she had made a decision to continue with life – to be happy. She didn't have access to language that would allow her to share succinctly with others her deepest thoughts and emotions. When I had initially thought of therapy, I had debated its worth for her because of her limited communication style. But she found a way to help us to understand what she was thinking and feeling. She did it with music – the universal language.

Throughout Jaime's life she has taught me so much and once again she was my mentor, my guide. We were ready to encounter another change. Jaime was fully ready to turn away from the past and to move forward.

The awe of the moment continued to hold me speechless. I reached out my arms to Jaime who remained perplexed at the silence after her presentation. She was curious to know if I "got it." I definitely got it – she had made a choice to live again – the way she has lived her entire life – through the ups and downs, fears and doubts, grief and pain, Jaime has always chosen love, hope, faith, and happiness.

What lay ahead? What unexpected twists and turns will be in our future? It really doesn't matter. My child, this amazing spirit, that I have had the privilege to live with, to share my life with, will be leading the way. She said all that needs to be said about our life together and life in general, "I Be Happy – Now!"